Hooked

A.J. NORRIS

ISBN: 978-1-7320238-7-1

Cover Design by: deliciousnightsdesign.com

Editing by: C.K. Brooke

ACKNOWLEDGMENTS

Thank you to my readers.

Chapter One

Kane

Prison sucked a big fat one.

I took my tray and sat at the end of my usual table in the cafeteria. I guessed if this was a school lunchroom, it would be considered the reject's table. I didn't care. My meal buddies consisted of a chubby guy who mumbled to himself, a dude who never made eye contact, and a man who growled when he ate. But they all had one thing in common—they left me the fuck alone.

The evening meal was a blob of unidentifiable meat, boxed potatoes, and waxy green beans. Oh, and for dessert, a scoop of indigestion.

Man, I needed to get out of here, except this place was my home for seven more years. I often fantasized about my fiancée, Jordana, waiting for me, then resuming our lives together after I got out. The reality was different, though. I was sent to prison for protecting her; the problem was that I couldn't tell anyone, including her. So, instead of pining for me, she hated me.

Yeah, prison wasn't the only thing that sucked.

I wanted to serve out my time in this hellhole peacefully. Keep my head down and mind my own business. Unfortunately, my fellow inmates had other plans.

While taking a bite of my barely-fit-for-human-consumption dinner, one of the inmates, whom everyone called "Monster," thumped the back of my head with his tray. I bit my tongue. *Goddammit.*

A week had passed since he'd last attempted to pick a fight with me. My bruises had only faded a day ago. Why the hell did he always choose me as his target? Okay, maybe I did know, but come on. Weren't we all in this together?

The evening's meat product, along with the watery gravy, spilled from his food tray down my shirt. I closed my eyes and swore under my breath. Should I ignore him? Yes. Did I want to ignore him? Without a doubt. Could I ignore him? No. Unfortunately, this would give everybody else a reason to think they could slop their food all over me.

All right, time to get it over with because, sooner or later, we were going to fight whether I wanted to or not. And I didn't. But he was never going to leave me alone.

"The fuck's your problem?" I jumped up from the table.

"You." He sneered.

"Go fuck yourself." Yeah, I know I said it. I wanted to get this dance over with quickly. I had better things to get back to, like staring at the walls of my cell or twiddling my thumbs. Real fun stuff.

Monster lunged at me, swinging his arms. I ducked and threw myself at his waist. The man-beast was a couple inches taller and had about sixty or more pounds on me, which said a lot since I was six-four. We both fell to the floor. See, I was preparing for a moment like this—one where I had the advantage. I landed on top and punched him in the face. The other inmates formed a ring around us, hooting and hollering. Blood sprayed from Monster's nose and his lip split as I threw punch after punch. I wasn't letting this asshole get in a jab. I learned from our past fights not to let up even for a second. Once he connected one of his giant paws with my face…it was lights out for me.

I kept hitting him until two guards pulled me off. I bucked against their hold. They slammed my torso across a table, wrenching one of my arms behind my back. My cheek hit the cold metal with a bang.

Sonofabitch!

On my left, Monster was in the same position as me. Hand behind his back. Cheek smashed into the table. He mouthed, *Fuck you.*

I snarled back.

The guards cuffed and yanked me upright. Like all the other times, we were both headed to the Hole. Regardless of who started or ended the fight, you went to solitary. With Monster in front, the guards led us down a corridor toward our new cells for at least the next few days. We passed the general population cell blocks and made a turn down another corridor. The tiny cells that made up the Hole were in a brightly lit area away from all the other prisoners. Despite the blood leaking from Monster's nose, the guards hauled him to a stop at the first of the tiny cells and shoved him inside the cramped space. He yelled, "You're dead, Kane Adler," before the door shut. He continued cussing me out, albeit now muffled through the metal.

They marched me to the next cell and unlocked the door.

"Warden wants Kane in his office," a male voice chirped over one of the guards' shoulder radios.

Oh, great. What now? All I wanted was to lie on the cot inside this cell. Alone. My cellmate snored. A couple of nights of peace sounded like a luxury.

Later, after a long walk through the prison, I was seated across from the warden, Mr. Maddox, in his office. While I waited for him to get off the phone, I noticed his desk was spotless. Who didn't have some papers on their desk? A Post-it? Folder? Nope. The warden kept a clean office. Even the file cabinets had nothing on top of them. No framed pictures. No plant with the last of its leaves clinging to life.

Maddox hung up the phone. He clasped his hands atop the desk. "Let's get right to the point, Mr. Adler. I don't like you."

I snorted. Was this statement supposed to bother me? "I'm touched, but not many here do. Is this why you wanted to see me?"

"No." He shook his head. "I'm sick of my COs having to deal with all your bullshit fighting." I considered reminding him that I never started even one of those fights. He wouldn't care, though. "Now you're going to be someone else's problem. You're being transferred immediately. First, you'll pack whatever personal belongings you might have; then, you will be escorted to a bus for transport upstate."

"Right now?"

"Bus leaves in twenty." He waved dismissively like I was one of those annoying swarms of gnats that inevitably got in your mouth as you walked through it. "Now get out of my sight."

What in the world? I wasn't the only one getting into fights. Monster was notorious for fighting. Then again, would a transfer be all that bad? One of the guards had given me shit every damn day since he started at the prison. I didn't even know what I did to that jackass. At least I wouldn't have to deal with him anymore.

Twenty minutes later, I was boarding a bus. A CO told me to have a seat at the front behind the metal cage partition separating the driver from the prisoners. I tugged at my handcuffs with my wrists as if I could break the chain connecting them. Although, I should've been grateful my ankles weren't shackled. A big bald man with a skull tattoo got on and sat across the aisle. He sneered at me then leaned his head back on the seat.

The engine started. I expected there would be more inmates on the bus. Instead, another guard trotted up the steps.

Oh, fuck.

Morrison, the guard who hated me, boarded the bus. A sick feeling settled in my stomach. He narrowed his eyes and plopped into a seat in the back. A second guard sat in front, sideways with his back against the window.

The bus lurched forward, waking my fellow

prisoner. We wound the path over some speed bumps and through a series of gates and out onto the road. The bus turned sharply, and I slid on the bench.

I situated myself for the ride by bracing my feet on the partition and floor. Then, like my travel companion, I closed my eyes with my head back and clasped my fingers to keep the cuffs from digging into my wrists.

I thought about what brought me to this point in my life. I never should have trusted him. My fiancée's father screwed me over because he wasn't man enough to own his sins and tell his daughter the truth. I ended up in prison for saving his ass.

Rain pelted the roof of the bus. I must've fallen asleep because, next thing I knew, a car horn blared. I looked out the window, left, right, behind. The bus swerved. I couldn't see what caused the driver to react. Gunshots rang out. The bus veered off the road onto the gravel shoulder, then back onto the pavement. More shots peppered the side of the vehicle. My fellow inmate crouched between the rows of bench seats. I covered my head with my hands.

We took on more rounds from an automatic weapon from the sound of it. A tire popped. Suddenly, we swerved sharply to the left. I held onto the bar on top of the back of my seat. The bus rolled. I lost my grip. My body smashed the wall then flew up as we flipped onto the roof. I lay on my stomach on the ceiling, which was now the floor. Blood ran into my eye. I ached all over, wondering if any bones were broken, and if so, how many. My wrists were still cuffed. The other inmate wasn't moving but moaned. Blood covered his face.

Morrison lay at the back of the bus. Blood poured out of the other guard. He had been shot. Most of the windows were busted out, including the one in the emergency exit door. I scrambled to the back of the vehicle, crawling on all fours. I didn't love the idea of waiting inside for the shooters to finish the job. That, and I hoped since the shooting stopped, the police escort had taken control of the situation.

Bars prevented me from exiting through the rear emergency exit window. I cranked the locking mechanism lever. The door wouldn't budge. I sat on my ass and kicked the metal panel with my feet. Finally, the door swung open. I peeked my head around the back of the bus. If anyone was still out there, I couldn't see them in the dark. At least the rain had stopped.

Fuck it.

I ducked through the small door—

"Where do you think you're going?" Morrison demanded. He was still lying down.

"If you haven't noticed, we were ambushed, and I'm not waiting in here for whoever to shoot me in the fucking head." I went outside and stayed low next to the overturned bus. I didn't have a clue where we were or how far we had traveled. Woods lined both sides of the two-lane road. Moonlight glinted off the broken glass littered all around. Why weren't we on the main highway? I couldn't see even one road sign or streetlamp. What happened to the shooters? The police escort? There was no one around that I could see.

What the hell?

I walked a few paces away. Glass crunched beneath my soft-soled shoes. What I wouldn't give for a pair of boots right now. No way the glass wasn't tearing up these flimsy-ass slip-ons.

A gun fired behind me. I dropped to the ground and rolled into the grass. A man dressed in all black appeared, passing in front of the headlights. He held a gun in his hand. A flashlight in the other. "You couldn't have gone far," he said. "Where are you?"

He shined the flashlight in my direction. Thankfully, the beam of light missed me by mere inches. I crawled backward on my stomach. Although I wasn't one with nature, the woods looked more promising for my survival than letting the shooter find me.

"Kane, where are you hiding?" The man was facing the opposite direction.

I crept farther from the road, past the tree line. The shooter pivoted.

He shined his flashlight directly on my face.
Shit.

I sprang off the ground and ran into the woods. He fired shots, the bullets hitting trees and whizzing past me.

I wasn't sure how long I'd been running when he gave up the chase. My legs burned and I was out of breath. I stopped and bent at the waist, gasping for air. When I could breathe reasonably again, I scanned the area for possible clues to where I was.

I heard something. Was that rushing water? I concentrated.

Whish…whish…whish…

Not water. I ran toward the sound.

Chapter Two

Kane

It was the sound of high-speed traffic. I came up to a cement barrier on the side of a highway. Up ahead, I saw a hotel and restaurant signs lit up above the trees. They had to be next to an exit ramp.

My mouth was so dry I couldn't think straight. My legs were on fire, and I had blisters on my feet. Then I saw the holy grail—a sign for a truck stop.

With what little energy I had left, I sprinted toward it. Ran up a steep hill on the other side of the exit ramp. Rushed across two lanes of traffic and into the truck stop parking lot. While I weaved my way between and around semi-trucks, I pulled off my orange prison-issue shirt and left it hanging across my cuffed wrists, although I knew this wouldn't fool anyone. Even if someone could overlook my orange pants, white sleeveless shirt, and pull-on shoes, the name of the prison I escaped from was stamped in black down each pant leg. Hardly inconspicuous. Oh, and let's not forget about the dried blood on my face.

I leaned against the side of a truck, the last of my energy zapped. The driver got out of the cab and slammed the door.

Shit. I was so fucked.

He was an older man who appeared to be in decent shape. "Looks like you've had a bad day," he said. He rested his right hand on the butt of a gun holstered at his hip. I sensed he wanted me to know he could shoot me if the need arose.

"You could say that."

He nodded at my clothes. "You escape or something? Because I doubt they let you take the uniform home with you."

My urge to run was squashed by my inability to make my legs work. "If you're going to call the police, can you just do it? I physically can't move anyway." I was in good shape, but I'd just run for miles right after a major bus accident. So, there was that.

He eyed me sideways for the longest time. "What were you in for?"

I could've lied. I thought about it. Something told me this guy would see through the thickest of bullshit, so I told the truth. "For driving a car." Okay, I grossly underplayed my crime. No one was sent to federal prison for driving.

"Last I checked, driving a car isn't illegal."

"It is if you're driving bank robbers away from the bank they just robbed." Shit, that might have been too honest.

The man whistled. "Makes sense. But why not get

a real job and be a law-abiding citizen instead?"

A sharpshot of regret hit me in the gut. "I had one and I was one. Long story."

"Ever kill anyone?"

"No, sir."

"How'd you get the nasty cut on your head?"

"Bus accident. I was being transferred to another prison."

"Is that how you escaped custody?"

"Yeah, but it's not the reason. Someone was trying to kill me, so I ran."

"Seems fair if you were running."

"I ran *because* he was shooting at me. The shooting happened first."

He cocked his head. "Why were you being transferred?"

"For fighting with another inmate."

"What for?"

"You've never been to prison, have you?" I grinned.

"Sure haven't, but I'm no saint." The trucker chuckled, giving me the suspicion that he simply hadn't been caught at whatever made him "no saint."

"So, you're saying the inmates fight to fight, that right?"

I nodded. "They'll use any excuse to beat someone's ass."

"Did you start it?"

"I ended it." I was starting to wonder if this guy was stalling and already called the police before he got out of the truck.

He pursed his lips. "Think anyone's looking for you yet?"

"I was wondering the same."

"I haven't heard anything come through on the radio." With his hand still on the butt of his gun, he cocked his head and squinted as if contemplating whether I was a danger to him or not.

I couldn't take the tension in the air. "Uh, so what are we doing here?"

"Where're you headed? I'm assuming you need a ride."

"South." I'd figured out from the road signs I was about a hundred and twenty miles north of where I wanted to be. Whom I needed to get to. And she wasn't going to be thrilled to see me, if she even would see me. But Jordy was the only one I could trust to help me. Would she betray me a second time, though?

"What's south?"

"Someone who can help me figure out who's trying to kill me."

He raised an eyebrow. "Yeah, you mentioned that. Would you say if you went back to prison now, without this knowledge, it would be detrimental to your health?"

"Good as DOA."

"I can't have that on my hands. All right. Come on," he said, turning toward the cab of his truck. He waved for me to follow. I lumbered after him—my brief rest against the truck had stiffened my muscles. I groaned under my breath with every step.

"If you're going to shoot me, can you do it in the head so it's quick? I usually wouldn't mind suffering, but I've already had a long day."

He chuckled. "Get in the truck before I change my

mind.”

"So, you are planning on shooting me?”

"Are you planning on killing me?”

"No.”

"Then let's agree not to kill each other, okay?”

"Deal.”

I went around to the passenger side and climbed in. It took every ounce of effort getting up those steps. The handcuffs didn't help either.

Wow. The truck was completely tricked out with leather seats and wood trim. I glanced over my shoulder. There was a bed above a table for two. "Nice truck.”

"She's a beaut.”

"You wouldn't happen to have a paperclip, would you?”

The man smirked. "What kind, jumbo or regular?”

"Jumbo, if you have it.”

Opening a compartment in the dash, he pulled out a folded stack of papers. He took one of the many paperclips from the pile and handed it to me.

I straightened out the thin piece of metal and inserted the end into the lock. I bent the clip a bit and released one of the cuffs, then the other. "Thanks.” I rubbed the bruises on my wrists. Man, they weren't the only things bruised either. Both my elbows were black and blue and scraped to shit. "How far south are you going? Anywhere near Westville?”

"Passing right through.”

"Good. You can drop me there.”

"What's your name, kid?” All right, I wasn't a kid at thirty-two years old, but in comparison to him, I probably seemed like one.

"Kane."

"That's not fake, is it?"

"Nope"

"Do you usually trust perfect strangers?"

I shrugged. "No, but I figured you could smell bullshit."

He laughed. "Good call. My name's Ray."

"Nice to meet you, Ray." We shook hands and he started the engine.

* * *

About an hour into the trip, the lights of several police cars flashed, lighting up the dark road ahead. "What's this shit now?" Ray said. "Why are we stopping, fellas?" The truck's windshield wipers couldn't keep up with the torrential downpour, blurring the cause for the traffic backup. He hard braked and I braced my hand on the dashboard. The semi shuddered and the brakes squealed. With the heavy rain, I anticipated skidding into the cars in front of us. However, Ray was clearly a skilled driver, and I avoided a second crash that night.

Fear prickled all over my body. "Is there an accident?" I prayed this was all it was—a simple traffic investigation. Except, by now, my escape would be all over police scanners and a BOLO would have been put out.

Ray radioed to another trucker who was closer to the flashing lights. Although I heard what the other trucker said, Ray repeated him. "He says it's a seatbelt check."

"Yeah, right. They're looking for me."

"Probably. You like baseball?"

"Um," I swallowed, "yeah, why?"

"Ever play?"

"As a kid I played travel ball. Now…well, I used to be on a softball team with my fiancée." What did this have to do with anything?

"Fiancée, huh? The one whose help you want?"

"Yeah." My heart pounded. We were getting closer to the police cars.

"Go in the back. There's a cubby with a ballcap and T-shirt from the last Dodgers game I went to. I can't do anything about the pants so if we have to get out, I'm really sorry."

I jumped from my seat. "Nothing you have to be sorry about. You got me this far."

"You'll see. Oh, and wipe the blood off your melon. Should be some water bottles and paper towels back there."

"I see them. Thanks."

I snagged a blanket for my lap and returned to my seat with a clean face, wearing the new hat and shirt. Sweat stung all down my back. Nothing like cutting it close. A cop flagged the truck over to the side of the road. I took a deep breath and stared out the side window.

Ray buzzed his window down. The rain pelted the cop's plastic covered hat. "Good evening, Officer. Some shitty weather we're having, huh?"

"Tell me about it. I'm soaked. May I see your license and registration, please?" Ray handed the cop his papers. The cop clicked on a flashlight, examining them. "Mind me asking where you're headed?"

"Home. Just dropped off my last load for the week."

The cop shone his flashlight into the cab. "Who you got with you? Pick up a stray?"

"Naw, are you crazy? I wouldn't pick up any hitchhikers. He's my son. We drive together."

"Can I see some ID?" the cop asked, shining the light on me.

Fuck. I glanced at Ray.

There was a moment of hesitation that seemed to last an eternity. The pouring rain and the diesel engine idling made a lot of noise, but nothing was as loud as the beating of my own heart. If I got taken into custody, then okay. But I didn't want Ray arrested for harboring a fugitive. I should've thought this through when I took the ride. *Dammit.*

"Well, Officer, I have it right here." My new best friend took a license from the visor and gave it to the man.

Man, I hoped I resembled his son. Or this situation was going to get way more fucked up than it already was. "Why do you have it?" the cop asked.

"Easy access. Like I said, Rodney and I drive together."

The cop studied the ID then my face. Back to the ID. He flipped it over. Okay, I must look a lot like his son. Was that why Ray had agreed to give me a ride? Had something happened to Rodney for him not to have possession of his own license?

The cop handed Ray back all the documents. "You've lost some weight, haven't you?"

"Yes, sir. I've been working out," I said.

He nodded. "We could use someone like you on highway patrol."

Could you? You don't know anything about me. I nodded. "That would be an interesting career change, but I'm going to stick with driving with my pops for now." I cuffed Ray on the shoulder.

The cop's eyebrows knitted together.

Did he see the bruises on my arm?

"Is everything all right here?" he asked Ray.

"Yes, sir. We're just trying to get home at a decent hour."

"All right, drive safe."

"What's this all about, anyway?"

Fuuuck me, Ray. The cop was going to let us go.

"An inmate escaped custody. Highway Patrol is doing checks on all major roads heading south. We don't think he'd come this way. But just in case, don't pick up any hitchhikers."

"No, sir. Is he dangerous?"

"It's presumed he's armed."

Like hell I am.

"Well, I'll keep on the lookout and if I see him—"

The cop nodded. "All right. Have a good night." He backed off and waved us through.

Ray wasted no time pulling back onto the road. He shook his shoulders like he had the willies. "I hate cops."

"He was just doing his job. Thanks, by the way. I owe you twice."

"You don't owe me anything." Ray stayed quiet for a few miles. "When I first saw you, I must admit that I got out of my truck because I thought you were my son. It would be impossible, but a father always hopes."

"What happened to him?"

Ray glanced at me. His eyes were watery. "I don't really know. He disappeared a year ago. Left his apartment and never came back. He didn't even take his wallet. I thought maybe he got arrested and thrown in jail somewhere."

"Did the police suspect foul play at all?"

"Nope."

"Huh?" *What kind of bullshit lazy-ass investigation is that?* "Is that why you hate cops?"

"Yeah. None of them ever did anything about my son. Told me he must've committed suicide. Uh-uh. No way. Not my boy."

"I'm sorry. That's gotta be tough."

"Believe me, you never want to lose a child. You have any kids?"

"Not yet."

He nodded. "When you do, keep 'em close and tell them you love them every day."

God, I wished I was in a position to help Ray. Unfortunately, now wasn't the time. "You mind if I have a peek at Rodney's license?"

He handed the ID to me. *Jeez.* He did look a lot like me. A few inches taller according to the license, and a bit lighter hair, though. Yet if you didn't know any better, and given the bad quality of the picture, it wasn't surprising the Highway Patrolman made the mistake.

An hour later, we pulled into a truck-friendly gas station a few miles from the house I'd shared with my ex-fiancée. Ray handed me a fifty. "What's this for? I don't want your money."

"I'm giving it to you anyway. Here, now take it. You can thank me by staying alive."

"Thank you. I'll try my best. I won't forget what you did for me, Ray, and I intend to return the favor. Don't ask me how, but I will."

"I believe you," he told me.

Seeing just how closely his son resembled me wasn't the only reason I'd asked to see the license. I'd wanted to know his last name. Javernick. I repeated it over and over while he drove away.

Chapter Three

Kane

With a clammy fist, I knocked on the front door of what used to be my house. On the walk from where Ray dropped me off, I passed the Westville Teachers Federal Credit Union. Their sign displayed the time of 12:26 AM. I didn't love the idea of waking up Jordy at this hour and scaring her, but what choice did I have?

I rapped my knuckles on the door again. This time, a light came on in the hallway that led to the bedrooms. Her silhouette appeared in the frosted window beside the door. "There better be a good reason you're banging on my door in the middle of the night or you're going to get a chest full of lead."

I smiled. She always had a way with words.

"I'm not even going to consider opening this door unless you tell me who you are. I have the police ready to go on speed dial and I have an itchy thumb."

"Jordy? It's me." My voice sounded like I had

gravel in my throat. "I know it's late and I'm supposed to be…" *In prison.*

"I don't know anyone named Me."

I sighed. "Jordy, please open the door."

"Kane?" she said with a tone of disbelief. "H-how is this you?"

"Long story. I need—"

"Aren't you supposed to be in prison? Don't tell me you escaped."

I rubbed the back of my neck. "It was an accident. I need your help. Please let me in and I'll explain."

"How do you accidentally escape from prison?"

"I had no choice. I was being transferred upstate and the bus was ambushed. They tried to kill me."

The door swung wide. Jordy had her arms folded across her chest and she gave me a once over. She looked exactly how I remembered her. Long brown hair, high cheekbones, slight cleft in her chin. Light hazel eyes with flecks of gold. After three years, I was concerned I'd gotten the details of her wrong in my dreams. We stood there staring at each other for God knew how long.

"Dodgers? I thought you were a Padres fan?" I removed the hat and touched my hairline. I hissed. The cut on my forehead was oozing blood.

She dropped her arms to her sides. "Oh, you're bleeding."

The change in her tone to utter softness turned my brain into mush. Jordy had a real girly-girl side to her that she didn't let many people see. I nodded, suddenly unable to speak. No one apart from Ray had shown me any kindness in years. And I certainly hadn't expected it from her.

"Does it hurt?"

"A little." I touched the gash on my forehead again and winced. My head swam.

She huffed softly and reached across the threshold. She pulled her hand back right before she made contact. "Looks like more than a little."

"I'll live. Can I come in? *Please.*"

"You shouldn't be here. I could lose my job or worse."

"I know. I'm sorry. And if there was anyone else I could turn to, I would." I was a complete asshole for showing up on her doorstep. Maybe I should've had Ray drop me off at the Mexican border. The position I put her in was unfair and beyond a dick move.

She swallowed and took a deep breath.

My chest tightened.

"Fine. But just so you know, I don't trust you."

"I know. I'm sorry."

"I don't think I ever will again." She stepped back and let me inside.

I brushed past her. "I know. I'm sorry."

"Please stop saying you know."

"I know you don't trust me, but you can." I glanced around the living room. Something was different. It wasn't new furniture. What was…? "You painted." I settled my focus on her face. A memory of us painting all the rooms before we moved in resurfaced. We had chosen the colors together. "What was wrong with the old colors?" I wasn't sure why I asked or even cared. And why did something as simple as her changing the paint hurt so badly?

"I wanted something new."

You mean something we didn't pick out together. I kept the comment to myself, nodding instead. "Do you live alone?"

She looked away. "If you're asking whether I'm single, then the answer's yes."

There was something hidden behind her answer, but prying seemed like a bad idea. She turned on a lamp next to the couch then sat down.

"Are *you* single?" she asked with a grin.

I chuckled quietly. Grateful for a break in the awkwardness. "I think you know the answer."

"I guess."

"You guess? You're all I thought about for the last three years. Yes, I'm single. Prison, remember?" I touched the wound on my head again. Pain spiked with each heartbeat. "Do you think I could wash up? I...I should probably get this wound cleaned out."

"Yeah." She stood and walked toward the bedrooms down the hall, keeping her head down, eyes on the floor.

I followed her, growing more curious by the second if she would lead me to the bedroom we once shared, or to the guest bathroom across the hall. She made a left into our bedroom. Her bedroom. I hated my life.

She'd redecorated. What was once blue and gray was now pink and gray. Honestly, the pink wasn't bad. It wasn't overwhelming. Soft. Subtle. And I'd give anything to lie in the king-sized bed with her. Not to have sex. Although yes, I wanted that. Fuck, I wanted her more than anything. But I wanted to hold her while we slept all night so I could finally get some rest. My stomach knotted. Standing right in front of her, I missed her like someone dying of thirst stuck in a desert missed water.

I tailed her into the master bathroom. "This is where I keep the first-aid supplies," she explained. Jordy bent over and removed a basket of first-aid stuff from under the sink. My eyes zeroed in on her curves. Before I could stop myself, a quiet groan slipped out.

She stood up and set the wicker basket on the counter. "What was that?"

"I didn't say anything."

"Oh, I thought I heard something."

"You might have heard me groan."

Her cheeks reddened. "Oh. Are you in pain or—? Yeah, not in pain." She may have been a tough cop, but she liked getting flowers and wearing dresses as much as she loved police work. No one at the Department knew the softer side of her. No one knew her vulnerable side. Her insecurities. What made her blush. And since she had been inexperienced when we met, no one knew all of her, except me.

"I am in pain." I cupped myself.

"Kane." She blushed harder. "That's not fair. I'm mad at you." I stepped closer to her. She put her hands on my chest and pushed until I was arm's length. "No. You don't get to come here and act like the last three and a half years didn't happen. You hurt me."

I backed off. My eyes focused on the floor that separated us. "I didn't have a choice. I had to protect you."

"I don't know what that means. There's always a choice."

"Does everything always have to be black and white with you?"

Her chin quivered like she was holding back tears. "You committed a major felony."

The room suddenly seemed more cramped. "No shit. I did it for you."

Confusion washed over her face. She narrowed her eyes. "You told me you were protecting someone."

"I was. You. And Eric." Although, I couldn't give two shits about her asshole father now.

A sob bubbled out of her throat. "We were happy."

"I never meant to hurt you, Jordy."

She held up her hand. "Don't do that. Don't say something cliché."

"Even if it's the truth?"

"You told me a thousand times you didn't mean to hurt me. After a while it's only words without meaning."

"And I also told you I was protecting you, which is the truth, even if you don't believe me. Fucking up our lives was the last thing I wanted to do."

"You still did what you did. The reason doesn't change anything."

"It should."

"If this was about protecting me, then what happened to the money, Kane? You know the money was never recovered. You have it stashed somewhere? Where is it?"

The bags the crew got in the car with from the heist were empty. I suspected the ones with the money had been switched outside the bank somehow and we were the decoys. I'd been told to wait around the corner until a certain time before pulling up to the bank. Anything could have happened. Any surveillance cameras in the area were conveniently under maintenance except for one. The one that could identify me as the driver. Was I their fucking scapegoat?

I tossed my hands up. "Beats the shit out of me. It was never about the money. You know what my cut was going to be?" I made a zero out of my hand and held it up. "Zip. Nada."

"Why did you do it then?"

Unbelievable. "I told you. They had hired muscle and they threatened your life."

"How did you even get mixed up with these people?"

I shook my head. "Eric got into trouble again and asked for my help. Things got fucked up from there."

"Why are you blaming my dad? He said he had nothing to do with it."

I sighed heavily. "I can't believe you really think he was telling you the truth. He's lied to you your entire life."

"Why did you even bother helping him out then?"

"Was I supposed to let him get murdered? Even he doesn't deserve that. And how would you have felt, had I let him get killed when I could've done something to prevent it?"

"I don't know." I believed that, too. Growing up with a father like hers had left emotional scars. In and out of prison. On drugs. Off drugs. Back on drugs. Missing birthdays and visitations. And all the excuses that came with his behavior. "I'm really sick of your hero complex. You ruined our lives."

Okay, she had me there. But, come on. "You know what? I shouldn't've come here. I'm sorry; I'll leave." She wasn't ready to believe the truth anyway. I was wasting my time.

"Where will you go?"

"What does it matter? I'm as good as dead anyway."

But what I didn't get was, why try to kill me now? I've never told the police or the FBI about what I knew about who planned the heist. Their names, descriptions, locations. How they hacked the city and bank surveillance systems. Would Eric be stupid enough to run his mouth?

I moved to the counter and riffled through the first-aid basket contents. What was I looking for? Oh, right, something medical. My hands shook. I hated fighting with Jordy. I felt her eyes on me. Judging me. "I'll take a couple Band-aids and go."

"That cut is going to take more than a Band-Aid. It needs stitches."

"And where would you like me to get stitched up? The hospital? Not an option."

"I don't know. Maybe you should have thought about—" She shut her mouth abruptly.

"Thought about what? The possibility of one day getting into a prison bus accident, escaping custody, and needing stitches? News flash: I'm not clairvoyant."

She held her arms rigidly at her sides, hands balled into fists. "You're right. You should leave."

"I am. Have a nice life."

I left the bathroom and kept going—never looking

back. I slammed the front door behind me.

* * *

Jordana

The front door slammed, rattling the house. I had followed Kane and stopped at the end of the hallway. He never looked back at me. I sucked in a breath. He took all the air out of the house with him.

Have a nice life. I wouldn't. Not even close. I swayed, suddenly too tired to stay on my feet, and lowered to the floor, deflating like a balloon. Part of me wouldn't've changed anything about the conversation we just had and was relieved he left. The other ninety-nine-point-nine percent had wanted him to stay.

I'd never forgotten the conversation we had in the interview room at the department before the FBI took over.

Kane sat up straighter when I entered the room. His eyes were red-rimmed and misty. I glanced at his cuffed hands anchored to the table. My heart panged. A tear leaked from my eye. As I pulled out the chair across the table from him, the legs screeched over the linoleum. I sat and placed my folded hands on the table. "Why would you—how could you do this to us?" I fought back more tears, trying my best to keep my composure, as I always did. I hated crying.

"You wouldn't understand."

"Try me."

"I had to protect someone, and this was the only

way."

"Who?"

"I can't tell you."

"Who could be worth going to prison over?"

He held his silence, and I knew why. He wasn't talking without a lawyer. We stared at each other because we both clearly realized this would be the last time we would be in the same room alone. I sat glued to the chair, hoping for a miracle. Perhaps this was a nightmare I'd wake from.

The door opened and in walked a woman with an FBI badge clipped to her waistband. "Officer Brooklyn, we'll take over from here." In other words, get the hell out of here before we have you removed. While I rose from my chair and backed out of the room, I kept my gaze focused on Kane.

Who could be worth going to prison over? Kane answered that question tonight, hadn't he? God, why was it so hard for me to trust him? I knew the reason and it had taken me three and a half years to realize I had my father to thank for my lack of faith in men. I was always waiting for Kane to disappoint me. So, when my dad told me Kane was going to commit a felony, my immediate thought was to shut him out.

And I fell right back into old habits again. *Goddammit.* Why had I told Kane to leave? I held a hand over my rolling stomach. I wanted to scream. Would I ever see him alive again? The rest of my body melted to the floor.

Chapter Four

Jordana

The doorbell rang.

Kane?

I sprang off the floor and ran to the front door. Peering through the cloudy sidelights, I made out two figures in dark clothing. They were talking back and forth. My shoulders sagged. What was I thinking? Kane wasn't coming back. I'd turned my back on him twice now.

"Who is it?"

"Officer Brooklyn?"

"Yeah? Who's there?" I asked, even though I already knew they were cops.

"White and Cruz from the Department."

I opened the door. My fellow officers, whom I played softball with, stood on my porch. White had his hand on the hilt of his gun. Cruz smiled awkwardly. He obviously didn't want to be here. "Hi." I tried to look surprised at having visitors so late. "What're you—?"

"Hey, uh, we were asked to come check out…" Cruz sighed. "Kane escaped custody tonight during a prison transport."

"He did? How?" My face warmed. Could they tell I was lying?

"He was being transported to another prison and there was an accident. Sorry I have to ask, but he didn't happen to come by here, did he?"

I shook my head. "No, he hasn't been here. I don't think—well, we haven't spoken in over three years. I don't think he would ever come here."

Cruz nodded. "I didn't think so either, but Chief insisted we ask. Sorry for bothering you at this hour."

"It's okay. I was still up."

White relayed the message through his shoulder radio that he and Cruz didn't find Kane or anything suspicious at my home. Yet, he still kept a hand on his gun. My heart sank to the floor. We had all been friends, once. Even if Kane were here, White would not need to pull his Glock. He wasn't a violent offender and always treated me with respect. This posturing on White's part made me sick.

"Are you still having trouble sleeping?" Cruz asked me while White finished radioing.

How did he know? *Oh, that's right.* I'd told him on one of the several dates we went on last year.

"Sometimes. Ava's at my parents' and the house is too quiet without her." My heart panged. I'd never told Kane about our daughter. At the time of his sentencing, I thought it was too cruel to tell him I was pregnant, and he wouldn't get to raise his child. He wanted kids. I also didn't want Ava to experience the same disappointment I went through every time my father wasn't there because he was in prison or off on another bender. Now I had to live with the guilt of my decision.

"How's she doing?"

"She's good. Thanks for ask—"

"Chief wants us to patrol the neighborhood," White said.

I wanted to tell them that Kane would be long gone by now. Although, in truth, he couldn't be more than a few miles, and that was if he was running.

"Well, you heard him, we'll be on our way." Cruz winked. "If you need anything, give us a shout."

"If you see him, you will call it in," White said.

Was that an order or a question? "Yeah." *I got it.*

Cruz rolled his eyes. "All right, White, she's not going to harbor a fugitive no matter who he was to her." He swept his hands at White, urging him off the porch.

I took a deep breath. Yeah, I'd already proven I was a heartless bitch when I had Kane arrested. Gawd. I guessed that was a good thing. No one would suspect me of protecting him. Betraying the love of my life a third time just wasn't in me, though. If he was telling the truth and someone was trying to kill him, then…

What was I talking about? He was telling the truth. Kane might not have told the FBI what he knew, but he wasn't a blatant, flat-out liar.

Cruz waved goodbye before he got into the driver's side of the cruiser. I shut the door before he could tell me to call him. We'd gone on five dates. Had sex once and he still was holding onto hope that we'd get back together. What he didn't realize was that I'd cried afterward. Kane had been the only man I'd been with up till then, and I'd been unfaithful to him. Of course, this was all in my head. We'd been broken up for two years by that point.

I dragged myself down the hall and crawled into bed. The mattress proved too hard and the pillow too flat. Restless, I rolled around, unable to fall asleep.

"What the hell," I growled.

I got up and slid the door wall open. A warm breeze blew the meshy curtain away from the screen. Inhaling deeply, the scent of lilac filled my nose. The motion-activated light came on. I yelped.

Kane slid from the shadows along the side of the house and filled the space I'd opened up. He smelled of sweat and the woods.

You came back. God, he seemed more massive standing so close to me. I couldn't see around him. I always loved how much bigger he was than me. A heady rush traveled my body. I stared at his muscular chest. Wanting his arms around me. Was this because I thought I'd never see him again, did him wrong, or did I just plain want him? Still? All right, I'd never stopped wanting him.

"White and Cruz were here a little bit ago, looking for you," I whispered.

Kane nodded and indicated with a gesture for me to let him in.

I unlocked the screen door and stepped aside. Keeping his eyes averted, he entered. He said nothing and I didn't want him to. I had questions, though they could wait. He peeled his shirt off and dropped it on the floor.

"I'm sorry about before," I said.

He stepped in front of me. His face was hidden in shadow. "Never apologize for speaking your truth."

"That wasn't my truth. I don't know what that was. I—"

"Shhh." He captured my face in his hands and kissed me. His touch made my pulse race and body quiver. I slid my palms up his muscular back. His body warmed my hands. "You should be angry with me."

"I'm not anymore. Truth is, I stopped being mad a long time ago. But when I saw you, it stirred up a lot of emotions."

"I get that. I'm a fucking mess, too. I miss you *so much.*"

"Why did you come back?"

"I couldn't leave things the way they were, especially not knowing if I'll survive past tonight."

"I wish you wouldn't say things like that."

"Even if they're true?"

"Especially if they're true."

One of his hands slipped around to the nape of my neck. He pulled me closer and every hard inch of him pressed against me. I gasped, tingling between my legs. Maybe after three years apart with no contact, the furthest thing from my mind should be lying with him. But it wasn't. Taking his hand from around my neck, I led him to the bed.

"No, Jordy. This isn't why I came back here."

"You don't want to be with me?"

"I didn't say that," he said, holding my hand in both of his. "I'm dirty."

"You're a bit smelly but it's okay."

He chuckled softly. "Not that—well, yeah, but I've got nasty prison filth all over me."

I smiled. "Okay, take a shower first. I'll get you a clean towel." I returned from the hall closet and set a clean towel on the bathroom counter.

"Thanks." Kane stood in front of the mirror, inspecting his head wound.

"You got cracked pretty good. Let me see."

He pivoted and rested his butt on the counter. I tilted his head down so I could get a better look and hissed. "This is going to sting when it gets wet. Unfortunately, I'm thinking the best way to clean it out is in the shower." There was a lot of dried blood, making it difficult to determine how deep the cut went. What I could see made my knees weak.

"How bad is it?"

I teased him with a gagging noise.

"All right, I get it. Let me get this over with." He stood to his full height, leaned into the stand-up shower, and turned on the water. For a master bath, the room was tiny. I stepped to the door to give him privacy, of which I'm sure he hadn't the luxury in prison. "No, stay in case I pass out from the pain."

I put the toilet lid down and sat.

He hooked his fingers in the waistband of his prison-orange pants and stripped them off. Underneath, he wore tighty-whities. Also prison-issue. I smiled. "I like your underwear."

He snort-laughed and got rid of them. "Feel free to burn this shit."

My mouth dropped open. Even though I had seen him naked plenty of times, he seriously had been lifting weights. A lot. And doing a million crunches a day. He now had a perfectly chiseled, V-shaped torso. Why did he have to look even better after three years of incarceration? Shouldn't he be a raggedy hot mess? Instead, he was plain hot. I put my hand out to feel his abs, which looked like they were carved out of marble. He put his hand on the back of mine and smoothed my palm down his chest and abs. He released my hand before we went any lower. Oh, God, why did he have to get involved in a bank robbery and screw up our lives? Why did I still want him? I bit my bottom lip.

"What happened to the orange shirt that goes with the pants?" I asked.

He chuckled. "Long story. I got a ride from a trucker and left it in his cab," he said, stepping into the shower.

Oh. "I was wondering how you got here," I said loud enough for him to hear me over the water. Driver must've been crazy, considering he was dressed in prison garb. But Kane did have the face of someone you could trust. Handsome with kind blue eyes and a warm smile, even with the deep gash on his forehead. I always thought he was much better looking than me. Like we were a mismatched couple, and people—other women, mainly—would wonder why he chose me. I didn't think I was homely, merely that he was out of my league. However, over the course of our relationship, he made me feel beautiful, so my insecurity faded.

"Yeah, I owe the guy my life. He literally saved my ass."

"Do I want to hear that story?"

"Probably not." He stepped under the spray.

"Fuck! That hurts!"

I cringed. "Told you it would sting."

"My head's on fire."

"You've been lifting weights?" I asked as a way of distracting him.

"Yeah, well, there's nothing much else to do other than play cards and watch TV, plus I was tired of getting my ass kicked."

"You aren't surprised, are you?"

Not wanting to sit there staring at him, I closed my eyes and listened to the water splash against the glass enclosure.

What seemed like twenty minutes later, he emerged from the shower. I handed him the towel from the counter, and he dried off. Then he slung the towel over the shower door. "I'd put something on, but…"

Our eyes met. I swallowed hard.

His brow furrowed. "Are you okay?" He smiled lopsidedly.

"I'm fine. It's just weird seeing you. You should spray some antiseptic on your wound." I edged off the counter and retrieved the bottle from the basket. "Use this."

"Thanks." He wiped the foggy mirror with his hand then leaned in and sprayed his head. He groaned. "Well, this is going to scar bigtime."

I shrugged. "It's a battle wound. It's kinda sexy."

He snorted. "If you say so."

"Since when are you so vain? Oh, I might still have some butterfly stitch bandages." I combed through the basket and found a strip of two. "Sit on the toilet lid so I can patch you up." After I placed the butterflies, he took my hand and kissed the back of it. "It's not perfect but it'll do."

"Anything is better than a gaping wound." Kane stood and we filed back into the bedroom. "I can sleep across the hall…if you want."

I froze. "No," I said, a little too forcefully. I wasn't ready to explain why that room was decorated for a little girl. She had a stuffed animal collection that rivaled an actual zoo and a purple frilly chenille bedspread that my mother had made for her, not to mention all the toys.

Confusion crossed his face and he smiled. "Okay."

"I mean, you don't have to. There's plenty of room here." *In our bed.*

A gap was growing between us. Where had the chemistry gone?

* * *

Kane

I stood naked in the bedroom next to the bed we once shared, mentally kicking myself for insisting upon a shower. Granted, I was nasty and stinky, but still. I ruined any chances of making love to Jordy. Possibly ever. Except for tonight, I couldn't see us ever being in the same room together again.

While we were in the bathroom, I couldn't stop stealing glances of her. And that's what I was doing too. Stealing. My future only held the promise of more prison time or death. I didn't have the right to even look at her.

Jordy came over to my side of the bed and sat. I kneeled between her legs, putting my hands in her silky long hair. She usually wore her hair in a bun, so anytime it wasn't pinned back was special.

"You've always liked my hair down."

"Uh-huh. I always wished you wore it down more." The strands slipped through my fingers. I smelled the shampoo she used.

"Do you want to get into bed?"

"Yeah. I'm naked, though."

I couldn't see her face well in the darkened room, but I heard her smile. "Would it make you feel better if I was naked too?"

"It would."

She giggled then pulled at the hem of her shirt. The cotton T-shirt fell to the floor. She shimmied out of her pajama shorts and panties. "There. Now I'm naked, too."

"I *do* feel much better."

Jordy lay on the unmade bed, leaving the blanket at her feet. I got in and lay next to her on my side. My hard cock poked her hip. "I didn't mean—sorry." Although we were both naked, sex wasn't a given, and I would never take something she wasn't willing to give.

"Kane?" she said softly. "You can say no, but will you—? God, I have no business asking you this. Will you make love to me?"

I licked my lips and swallowed. "Um, yeah." Why in the world did she ever think I'd say no? I put my hand on her belly and she moved it toward her breasts. Except I wanted my mouth there instead. Latching onto one of her breasts, I flicked my tongue over and around the nipple. She gasped and arched her back. I slid my hand between her thighs and worked my way up. Her legs parted, allowing me full access. I massaged her clit with my thumb and pushed two fingers inside. She was so hot and wet my head spun. My mouth left her breasts for a moment to kiss her on the lips. "I love you." I wanted to hear her say those words, too, although I didn't expect them.

Unable to wait any longer, I settled between her legs. My cock bumped against her opening. Then my brain caught up to what was about to happen. How could I risk getting her pregnant when my life was nearly over? I couldn't imagine how I was going to survive this dumpster fire alive.

"Jordy, do you have protection?" I didn't want to think about what it meant if she said yes. We hadn't used condoms in a while before I went to prison, because we'd wanted a child. Although we hadn't been actively trying, per se, we weren't *not* trying, either. So, if she had condoms now, that meant—oh god…

"In the nightstand next to you."

I'd loved the idea that I was the only man who'd been inside her. I squeezed my eyes shut and shook off the jealousy building in my heart. Whatever my feelings were on the subject, she had the right to do what she wanted.

I fumbled blindly in the drawer, managing to find an open box of condoms. Grabbing one of the square packages, I ripped the foil with my teeth and rolled it on. I plunged inside her.

She whimpered and locked her arms around me.

I groaned with every thrust. I was so fucking close to coming I stilled to stifle my orgasm. She knew what I was doing too and rotated her hips. "Stop that, baby, you're going to make me come."

A giggle escaped her mouth.

I put her legs on my shoulders and rolled her up, so she couldn't move her hips around. I thrust deeply, getting into the steady rhythm she loved.

She moaned in ecstasy and clutched my arms—what she did every time she came. Hearing the sounds she made, the way her body felt beneath me, sent me straight over the edge. I shouted and came hard.

I prayed the condom didn't break.

Chapter Five

Jordana

The night we conceived Ava was when I felt the closest to, and most in love with, Kane. Ava was three now. She loved my mom and stepfather. Our daughter, thankfully, had been spending a few days with them, giving me some much-needed alone time, which I rarely got as a single parent. Between work and raising her, I didn't have any time to myself. My mom got that, though. My father left us when I was Ava's age. So, she offered to babysit overnight a few days a month.

Kane had no idea I was five months pregnant when he was sentenced to ten years in federal prison. I tried telling him the one and only time that I visited him. But what was he supposed to do with the knowledge? He couldn't be there for any of the doctor visits or the birth. He wouldn't raise her. He wouldn't see any of her "firsts." First smile. First crawl. First step. First word. If that wasn't bad enough, I also deprived Ava of her other set of grandparents.

Keeping this secret felt like a betrayal. How would Kane react if I told him now? Should I even tell him? Would he hate me? I'd hate me.

For the first year he was incarcerated, I daydreamed about how I would've told him I was pregnant. Different scenarios, too. One rendition involved wrapping the home pregnancy stick like a present and having him open it. Another where I told him we'd have to move up our wedding date. He would ask why, and I'd say, "My dress won't fit if we wait six more months."

Kane lay on the bed with his eyes closed. He might have looked relaxed if it wasn't for the crease in his brow. I put my hand on his chest. Like I thought, he wasn't sleeping. He placed his hand atop mine. "Can't you sleep?" he asked.

"I'm trying. My heart is ping-ponging around my chest." Although, my stress wasn't just about what was going to happen to Kane. I pictured Ava. She had his blue eyes. Her bedroom was just across the hall, and he didn't even know it.

"Yours, too." Kane pulled me onto his chest and wrapped his arms around me. His body heat warmed me. He breathed deeply. "You smell good," he said softly.

"So do you."

He chuckled. "I smell like your shampoo."

"Well, I like the scent." I kissed his chest and rolled off him onto my back. He laid on his side and put his hand on my belly—the warm weight reminding me of being pregnant with Ava. "Kane?"

I whispered.

"Yeah?"

You have a daughter. "What's prison like?" Okay, not what I should've said.

"Like being trapped in a small box with only pinholes to breathe."

"You get to go outside, don't you?"

He snorted. "An hour and thirty a day if I'm not in the Hole."

"Why would you be in solitary? You're not a violent offender."

He took a deep breath. "If someone picks a fight with me, I'm going to defend myself."

"Maybe I'm naïve for saying this, but if you're only defending yourself, why—?"

"Doesn't matter who starts the fight; you both go down for it."

"That doesn't seem fair." Okay, yes, I was naïve.

"That's prison."

"Well, that sucks."

"And then some." Kane propped himself up on his elbow and leaned over me. He ran his fingers through my hair. Caressed the side of my face. His gentle touch made me want to cry. I imagined the droplets slipping from the corners of my eyes and down my temples. "I miss you so much."

I miss you, too. I nodded even though he couldn't see me well in the dark.

He pressed a kiss to my forehead. "I love you more than anything in this world. I'll always hate myself for what I did to us."

I blew out a breath. *I hate myself, too.* I should have stuck with him when he needed me the most. I should have told him about Ava.

Kane rolled to his back and put his arm behind his head.

I sat up. "Kane."

"Hmm?"

"I need to tell you something. I—we—" *We have a daughter,* played in my head on repeat. *Just tell him already.*

The doorbell rang. "Uh!" My heart sank.

* * *

Kane

Jordy jumped off the bed like she'd been zapped on the ass. "Relax," I said, "it's probably just Cruz and White again."

"I'm sorry, but did you just tell me to relax? How can I relax?" She opened the closet and pulled on the silky robe I'd gotten her for the last Christmas we spent together. It was good to see she didn't throw out at least one of the gifts I bought her. She wasn't wearing her engagement ring, I noticed.

The doorbell rang again. "Give me a second, will ya?" Jordy shook her head and glanced at me. "What do you think they want?"

I sighed. "Probably checking in with you. Why don't you answer the door and find out?"

She wrung her hands. "You should get some clothes on, or—I don't know."

"I don't have any clothes to put on." I was not about to put my prison issues back on. Speaking of which, I probably should have thought about that sooner.

"Your clothes are downstairs."

"I can't exactly go running through the house right now." So, it looked like I was hiding like an escaped convict. I snort-chuckled.

"What is funny right now?"

"I'm gonna hide like an escaped convict." I laughed again. "You see why that's funny, right?"

"No." She left the bedroom, clutching her robe together at the neck.

Now, where was I supposed to hide with no clothes on? The closet seemed the most logical place, which was exactly why I couldn't hide there. It would be the first place a cop would look. Under the bed wouldn't work since it was a platform.

I gritted my teeth and fetched the prison pants from the bathroom floor. I cursed, plugging my legs into the orange pieces of shit. Slipping outside using the door wall in the bedroom which led to the back of the house, I crept my way around to the side where it was darkest. The bushes provided additional cover. I stepped on a sharp twig in my bare feet and hopped on one foot, crying like a little bitch. I took a deep breath.

I heard two male voices speaking with Jordy on the porch. Cruz and White. I stayed out of sight, which also meant I couldn't see what was happening.

"Sorry. We're back," Cruz said.

"Oh, it's all right. I figured. Still not convinced Kane wouldn't come here?"

Cruz sighed. "I am. But the chief asked us to search your house."

"You have a warrant?"

"Uh, we have probable caus—" White started.

Jordy giggled. "I'm only kidding. Come on in, guys."

The screen creaked open.

"The department should be here in a bit to do a quick sweep…" Cruz trailed off as he went inside the house.

Dammit! Now I couldn't hear anything. *Quick sweep of what?*

A police siren went off. Two quick be-beeps so the officers inside knew they'd arrived. Blue and red lights flashed, glowing against the brick of the house next door.

I peeked my head around the corner. Two cops trotted up the front walk. The screen door opened then slammed shut.

The neighbor's back porch light came on and their little white fluffy dog darted outside. Snowball sniffed around. I must've made a noise his canine ears picked up, because he ran toward me. I crouched down low behind the bushes. Snowball slowed and growled on the approach. This dog, who had known me well three years ago, barked.

"Snowy, shhh," I whispered. He pushed through the bushes. His tail wagged and he yipped. *I'm happy to see you too.* "Quiet, dog." I picked him up and petted him. Thankfully, this silenced him. The neighbor whistled and Snowy squirmed. I put him down but he stayed by my side. I pushed his little butt. Snowy glanced back at me. *Go,* I mouthed and waved him away.

The neighbor's slippers appeared under the brush. "Snowy," he called. "Snowball. Where are you?"

I gave the little furball another gentle shove.

"Where did that rascal go?" Steve, the neighbor, paced back and forth. "I know you came over this way."

All right, this dog did not want to leave. He yipped again.

The slippers halted right in front of where I was squatting. *Shit.* I held my breath. "Snowy! Git over here." This time I pushed the dog into the bushes, hoping he'd take the hint and go the rest of the way on his own. He wiggled through. Thank god.

"There you are," Steve said, picking up his dog. "Did the police scare you? Is that why you were hiding? They're probably some of Jordana's friends from the department. Nothing to be worried about."

Okay, dude. Move along.

Gawd. I was a grown man hiding in the bushes. This was what my life had come to? Sneaking around my own house?

"Sir, you need to get back inside," White called to the neighbor.

"What's going on?"

Cruz's partner approached and Snowy growled. *Good dog.* I never liked Officer White. The neighbor made no effort to quiet his dog. He started barking.

"What's your name?"

"Steven Tiller. Is everything alright with Jordana?"

"She's not your concern."

"I'm the Neighborhood Watch captain. So, if something's wrong, then it is my concern."

"Congratulations, but you still need to get back in the house."

Snowy kept growling. He leapt out of Steve's arms, grabbed ahold of White's pant leg with his teeth, and yanked. White tried shaking the dog free and failed. Snowy growled and barked like he'd grown fifty inches and gained a hundred pounds while holding on. I bit my tongue to keep from laughing.

Cruz came around the side of the house. "From the sound of it, I thought you were being mauled by a large dog," he said, laughing.

"I am."

Steve made a half-assed attempt to call off his raging beast.

White's struggle continued. He bent and tried removing the dog with his hands. Snowy snapped at him. "Ouch, you fu—can you get your dog off me before I shoot it?"

"Knock it off, White, he's a little dog."

Steve easily gathered the pooch in his arms and carried him away. "I ought to report you for threatening my dog."

"Hey, do you want my badge number for your report?" White called after him.

What an arrogant SOB.

"Why are you like that?" Cruz asked.

"What? Dude's dog should be put down."

You're an idiot.

"The dog was all of ten pounds."

I hoped Steve did file a complaint against White.

The officers left the side yard. A few minutes later, their cruiser pulled away from the curb.

Were there other cops in the house? I stuck my head around the corner. The other vehicle was still there. God, I had to run. I hated that I couldn't say goodbye to Jordy. *Fuck it.* I had to see her.

I went back to the bedroom slider at the rear of the house, crouched down, and peered in. Only a light from the bathroom shone in the room. The bedspread was crumpled on the floor. The closet door was open, and clothes lay in a heap between the walk-in and the bedroom. Jordy was sitting on the bed. I tapped on the glass. Her face lit up when she saw me, then she frowned and came over to the door.

Jordy slid the glass slider open a crack. "You have to get outta here," she whispered. "There's no time."

"I, uh…I—" My heart pounded in my throat.

"It's okay. You don't have to say anything."

"I don't want to—" *Go.*

She shook her head. "Kane, I know, but the chief ordered a search."

"They know I'm here."

"They don't."

The *you-have-to-leave-now* was implied. I should never have come. Even though I kept repeating this to myself and knew leaving for good would be the best for her, I was a selfish bastard. I wasn't ready to let go.

She smiled tightly, without joy. Wasn't this whole thing a kick in the dick? My chest ached, or was it my soul?

"Be safe," she whispered. Her tone suggested this was goodbye.

I nodded and slipped out.

Chapter Six

Kane

Holding my breath on the back patio, I waited, checking for any sign of movement in the yard. Left. Right. Forward. Seeing nothing out of the ordinary, I hightailed it across the lawn. I leaped over the three-foot deep, slope-banked drainage ditch marking the edge of the property. In the field beyond a stand of overgrown saplings, trees, and bushes, a flashlight flitted around.

Shit.

I froze, then glanced behind me. Two patrol cars pulled up with their lights flashing.

Now what?

My best option was to go through Steve's yard. I took two steps and slipped on the dewy grass on the sloped bank, landing hard on my ass. I grunted. And slid into the water-filled ditch. I hissed through my teeth.

So cold.

The cool, murky water came up to the middle of my chest. I dragged myself to the metal drainage tube because I missed the opportunity to get the hell away from there. It was the only place to hide. The pipe was narrow but still wide enough for me to get inside. However, only a few inches of air space separated the water from the top. The inside of the tube was covered in slime. My hands and feet slipped on the sides of the tube, preventing me from getting any traction.

Forced to float on my back, I treaded water with my arms to keep my head above the surface. Normally, I wasn't claustrophobic. But with little breathing room and surrounded by water, I was having a difficult time staying calm. Panic prickled my entire body.

I sank to the bottom then came up gasping. Water went up my nose. Jesus, if I kept this shit up, I was going to drown. What I needed was a good deep breath, except there wasn't enough space.

A flash of light shone into the tunnel. A dog barked, except the sound didn't come from Steve's little ankle biter. This was the bark of a large breed. A canine cop. I took the deepest breath I could manage, which wasn't anywhere close to sufficient, and let myself sink to the bottom. Hopefully, the dark depths kept me hidden. Although, I didn't think anything could mask my scent at this point.

I pushed farther into the pipe, came up for air, and went under again. I held my breath for as long as I could. I'd read that, even if I happened to find something to use as an air tube, the pressure of the water around me wouldn't allow my lungs to expand.

No garden hose or reed would save me from drowning.

I opened my eyes. Dim light from a flashlight penetrated the surface and turned the dirty water above me yellowish-green. I held still. Air bubbled out of my mouth. I couldn't hold my breath much longer.

* * *

Jordana

After composing myself for some time, I went outside and stood on the back patio. In the dark, I couldn't get a count on how many cops roamed the field behind my house. Their flashlights flicked back and forth.

A police dog and its handler walked the length of the drainage ditch separating the backyard from the field. How had this night turned into a manhunt? One minute we were blissed out in bed, and the next, Kane was hiding somewhere. I only hoped he had time to get away from the neighborhood first. But given the way the dog was sniffing and whining, the Belgian Malinois must have caught his scent. It wasn't likely to give up until he found Kane unless forced.

Oh god, what if—?

A spike of fear stabbed my heart.

What if Kane was in the drainage tube? The pipe was almost filled with water. He could drown. If he died I, oh god…it was bad enough with him in prison, but knowing he wouldn't be alive anymore was unthinkable.

Why didn't this damn dog give up?

"I can't see shit in this water," the dog's handler said to another cop, who'd joined him at the bank of the ditch. *Willis.* Although I didn't know him well, I recognized his voice. He had one of those unmistakable voices that carried. The man also had a silent confidence. He didn't show off or pretend he was a badass.

"Too dark to see anything. Besides, if Kane's in there, he's probably already dead. No one can hold their breath that long," the other officer said. What an asshole. *Who is that?* I couldn't take the waiting. I shivered even though it was warm outside. I'd rather Kane not drown in shallow water. Prison had to be better than death. Of course, with a target on his back, how long would he last?

I strode across the backyard and up to the edge of the ditch. At Willis's command, the dog finally stopped whining and sat down at his feet.

"Ma'am, you should go back in the house. This is no place for a woman," the asshole said, not Willis. I didn't know this guy, but I already knew his type: assuming and arrogant.

Oh, hell no. So, if I were a man I could be outside? Misogyny much? I put my hands on my hips. "Excuse me, I'm a cop and this is my backyard. Why don't you leave my property?"

"That's not what I—"

"Meant? Well, that's what you said. In fact, all of you leave. I told you that Kane isn't here nor has he been. Now go!" Pissed off made a skilled liar out of me. How many felonies had I committed tonight?

Willis' eyebrows raised.

"You heard me." Okay, so I didn't have the authority to call off a manhunt, but my person was trapped underwater and possibly drowning, while they fucked around complaining it was too dark to see. Of course it was too dark to see. It was three o'clock in the morning.

"Why are you so defensive?" the asshole said.

"Because you're pissing me off." I glowered at Willis. "Will you tell your friend here that he's an idiot? I'm too tired."

Willis snorted. "I would but you're doing a fine job without my help."

"Thanks."

"She's right, you know. He's not here. Ratchet would've scented him by now."

I wasn't so sure this was true. His canine didn't quit whimpering until he'd made him heel.

Willis and Kane had been friends. Rumor had it, he visited Kane in prison several times over the last three and a half years. Would he protect him, though?

Willis checked in with the chief via shoulder radio, who squawked in return. "Chief says to call off the search for now."

"That's bullshit," the asshole said.

Willis shrugged. "Makes sense. We're wasting time. Brooklyn was the one who got him arrested. I highly doubt he would come here."

"Is that true? I heard you were engaged to marry him."

"It's true. We *were* engaged. Past tense. I hate him and he knows it." I cringed inside. The words felt like a foreign language coming out of my mouth.

Willis yelled to the other cops in the field to clear out. He pivoted toward the asshole cop. "You heard the order, beat it."

"What about you?"

"I'll be right behind you in a minute." Willis shook his head. "Asshole," he muttered under his breath when the other guy was out of earshot. We watched the idiot disappear around the front of the house. "Are you okay, Brooklyn?"

"Yeah."

His eyebrows knitted together. "Are you sure? I know if I just found out my fiancé escaped from prison, I'd be a little messed up over it."

"He's on his own." I turned my eyes toward the ground—anything to keep from searching the ditch for Kane. Was he even in there? I had a feeling he couldn't have gotten far.

Ratchet sniffed my leg then pawed the ground at my bare feet.

"Whatcha smelling, boy?"

Prickly heat spread throughout my body. Kane had been all over me. In me. Good thing the dog hadn't been in the house. The T-shirt he'd taken off was still on the bedroom floor.

Willis leaned over and patted Ratchet's side. "Take it easy. She's not who we're here for."

"Is he always like this?"

He shrugged one shoulder. "Eh, he's usually pretty chill. He's a bit antsy tonight." Willis averted his attention to the ditch and motioned toward it with a nod. "Something over there he liked, but he wouldn't point to it. So, I dunno. I thought maybe I saw…*some*thing in the drainage pipe, but Ratchet would've signaled if it was of the human variety."

The tension I'd been holding in my shoulders eased. Kane had gotten away. "Can I ask you something? Because I've always been curious…"

He smiled thinly. "What's on your mind?"

"Rumor has it, you visited Kane in prison a few times. Why?"

"We grew up together. I wanted to see if I could do anything to help him. I know he would've done the same for me."

"When was the last time you saw him?"

"It's been about a year. I stopped going because he made it clear he wasn't going to try and help himself. Frustrates the hell out of me. The thing is, what he got messed up in was so out of character, I didn't want to let it go."

"And now?"

"I haven't given up on him. He's like a brother to me. I had to step away for my own sanity. Can I ask *you* something?" He stared at my feet, or maybe just the grass between us. "Do you really hate him? It doesn't take a genius to figure out Ava's his. Unless she was four months premature, Kane's her father."

I nodded. "I guess the only person I fooled was myself, thinking no one would do the math."

"I never wanted to say anything and I haven't—not even to him. I don't think it's right, but that's between you two."

"I appreciate your silence. I…" I took a deep breath.

"Listen, I'm not judging you. I'm in no position to."

His statement made me curious. What was his

story? Although he'd grown up with Kane, they hadn't been close since their teens. So, I didn't know a lot about Parker Willis. He was single, as far as I knew, and lived alone with Ratchet. "Any idea where you think he might have gone?"

Willis shrugged. "Not really. He's still in love with you, so I wouldn't be surprised if he did show up here." He squinted in the darkness out into the field then turned and tilted his head, looking at me sideways. "Just so you know, I don't want anything to happen to him."

"Like what?"

"Being killed."

I inhaled sharply and my insides quivered.

"Sorry to be blunt, but if he's found, it could go very badly for him, and I don't think he deserves that. I don't think you do, either."

"Well, I don't want him to die."

He smirked.

"What?"

"You know, I'm good at reading people. I can see you're nervous. And I'm going to ignore the fact that you keep looking over at the ditch."

Shit. And here I thought I'd been so diligently not looking. "Am I? I didn't realize I was."

"No kidding. But like I said, I don't want to see him dead."

We stared at each other. He was protecting him, then? Wait… or was he trying to trick me? Perhaps Willis merely wanted to bring Kane in quietly and without incident. Be the hero. Not that he was the showoff type, seeking accolades. "Do you think I want that either? He hasn't been here."

Willis nodded. "I'll make sure the chief knows."

God, now I knew what people in movies meant when they said, "Trust no one."

Although, there was one person I could probably trust, because he'd been known to defy orders if he felt he was doing the right thing: Ryan Keith. The question was—and I hated myself for having doubts—was Kane telling the truth?

Only one person was available to ask, and that was my father, Eric Brooklyn, provided he would actually tell me the truth for once.

Chapter Seven

Kane

I crawled out of the ditch, coughing up dirty water, and collapsed on the sloping bank. Exhausted from nearly drowning, I lay on the ground, unable to move. A breeze drifted over me and I shivered. The house and Jordy were less than fifty feet away. I wanted to go to her, yet I couldn't put her at risk again. She had way more to lose than I did. Her career. Her freedom.

And what did I have to lose, other than my life? It wasn't as if I had any reason to live. Jordy would move on. Hey, I always liked Parker Willis. Maybe they would hit it off after I was gone. I only heard bits and pieces of their conversation while I was trying not to die but they seemed to get along.

Okay, what in the fuck was I saying? I didn't want her to move on. She deserved to be happy but, goddammit, the thought made me want to puke. If she'd been with anyone while I was in prison, I certainly did not want to know about it.

The sun began rising, light peeking through the trees. I imagined the UV rays were like poison and I'd burn up like a vampire. However, I'd settle for my pants drying. Of course, I didn't know what good that would do. They were orange and I had no shirt or shoes. Thumb. Sore. Me.

If I could get back into the house, I'd look for some clothes. Jordy couldn't have tossed everything. A hole in my chest formed. I winced. Man, I didn't know what was worse—her throwing out everything of mine, or my life reduced to boxes. Because none of my things had been in the closet or around the house that I could tell.

This led to thoughts of my parents. They had boxed up my childhood bedroom to make a crafting room for my mom. It was like being kicked out of the house even though I had moved out on my own years prior. Although losing Jordy was much worse. But man, should I call them to let them know I was alive? No, I wasn't involving them in the slightest.

You dumbass!

I should've gone directly to the FBI and not involved anyone. Who was the agent in charge of my case? Latasha something. She seemed like a reasonable person.

* * *

Jordana

My shift started in two hours, which didn't leave

me much time. I wanted to believe Kane's story so badly, yet doubt crept its snakes-for-hair head into my brain. I needed to hear what I already should believe without question, from Eric. I threw on my uniform and drove thirty minutes to the county lockup where my father was incarcerated.

Even though he had been in and out of prisons my entire life, I refused to get used to the idea of him being in one. I rarely told anyone he had spent a lot of time behind bars. A part of me believed he preferred three hots and a cot, though. At least then, he always had a roof over his head and knew when his next meal would be.

I pulled into my usual spot in the visitor's parking lot. My usual spot? I shouldn't have a usual spot at a prison. I ground my teeth.

Since I was a cop, the DOC officers let me see my father outside normal visiting hours. After I was patted down and all the other usual protocols completed, I was escorted to the room where most of the visits took place. The large space was set up like a cafeteria with tables and chairs. A couple of vending machines with sodas and snacks stood in the corner.

The steel door opposite me opened, and my father walked up and sat across from me at the table. He smiled sheepishly. He appeared more disheveled than usual, hair mussed, face scruffy with a weeks' worth of mostly gray stubble.

"What a nice surprise. This isn't your usual day for a visit."

"No, it isn't." I smoothed my hair against my scalp, even though it was tied back in a sleek bun. "How have you been?" I didn't want to start off with why I'd come off-schedule.

He shrugged. "All right. As far as prisons go, this one isn't half bad."

He was a connoisseur, apparently. I sighed and glanced at the ceiling. "The reason I'm—"

"How's Ava?"

"She's great. Eric, I need to ask you a serious question." I never called him "Dad."

"Your mom tells me she's quite the talker these days. Developing a personality."

My eyebrows knitted and I shook my head. "Wait a minute, when did you talk to my mom?"

He looked as confused as I felt. "She visits me every so often. I thought you knew."

Uh, no. This was news to me. Why on earth would she come see him at all? I didn't know they still spoke to each other.

He took something out of his breast pocket. "She brings me pictures of my grandkid. See." Between his middle and index fingers he held up a photo of my daughter with a big smile on her face. Her blue eyes were alive with carefree joy. I nearly shed tears. The guilt from last night over Kane not knowing about her returned. I put my hand on my belly.

"I didn't know my mom came here."

"Yeah, her and what's-his-face she's married to."

"You know his name. Robert's a good guy and Ava adores him. And he's good to my mom." *More than I can say for you.*

"I'll take your word for it." He cleared his throat.

"Eric, I need to know something important. Before the robbery, were you in trouble—?"

'What's new in the world of law enforcement?"

"Why are you trying to change the subject again? I need to know if you went to Kane for help. What kind of trouble were you in?"

"Did he tell you I asked for his help? I don't know anything about that bank robbery. And I certainly wouldn't ask someone who doesn't even like me for help." He ran a hand through his hair a few times.

I rolled my eyes. "That's crap. You *told* me about the robbery, so how can you say you knew nothing about it? You don't even remember your own made-up bullshit."

"Are you calling me a liar?"

I placed my palms flat on the table and leaned in. "I'm asking for the truth."

"I am telling the truth. I love you and would never have hurt you like that if it wasn't true, honey."

Since when did he call me "honey"? "Don't call me that. We've never had a close enough relationship for you to address me with *any* term of endearment. You've hurt me so many times, I've lost count."

"Dammit, Jordana!" He banged his fists on the table.

"Hey, watch it, Brooklyn," said the CO keeping watch over Eric.

"Apologies," my father said, raising his hands, signifying he was taking it easy. He leaned closer to me over the table and spoke quietly. "When are you going to stop giving me shit about my past mistakes?"

I crossed my arms over my chest. "Past mistakes? Are you kidding me? How about when you stop lying to me?" Apparently, I wasn't here because I had doubts about Kane's story. I was here to confront my father.

"Why would I want to break you and Kane up? He was good to you."

"I don't know why you want to hurt me. I've never done anything but try to love you. Why you insist on making it so hard is a fucking mystery."

He stared at the table. Fiddled with a dent in the metal with his thumb. "I didn't lie to you about Kane taking part in the bank robbery."

"No, just left out the part that he only did it because of you."

"You don't know anything. I wasn't anywhere *near* that bank."

"Hmm, let's see," I said, putting a finger to my lips. "You knew what bank, what time, the date, and the getaway route. No. You had nothing to do with it. Stop lying. You're only making yourself look worse. Kane didn't confide in you. You went to him for help and got us all involved."

"You're not involved. Where are you getting this from?"

"Oh, so the bad guys didn't threaten my life, huh? Is that what you're saying? Kane wasn't trying to protect the both of us. He was doing it for the money?"

"Not all the money was recovered," he hinted. Trying to make Kane look guilty.

"Yeah, because you probably have it stashed somewhere."

He waved dismissively. "You've always had a vivid imagination."

"You are sick. I remember the night you told me

about the bank heist and Kane's involvement. You knew I'd caught you in another lie about what you did with the money we gave you for rent and couldn't face telling me the truth, so instead you played into my insecurities and let me believe my fiancé had gone dirty."

He mirrored my pose—arms folded over his chest. "I didn't buy drugs with the money you gave me. I swear."

"Then what did you do with it?"

Eric cast his eyes downward and mumbled, "I lost it."

"How did you lose five thousand dollars? That money was for all the back rent you owed so you wouldn't be kicked out of your apartment."

"I gambled it away. Is that what you want me to say?"

"If it's the truth. I'd rather you be honest with me. I get that you have problems. But the lying—I can't, I just can't."

"Well, I had to tell you something to get you off my back. You don't understand how judged I feel by you."

"Oh, this is my fault now? I'm responsible for your lies, your actions?" I stood. "You know I must be crazy to even entertain the notion that you could ever be truthful about anything. Your entire life is one big lie. You know what? I'm glad you weren't around much. And thank god I didn't turn out like you. And another thing: Do you like being in prison?"

His gaze flipped up to mine. "Of course not. And it's not my fault I'm here."

"It's not? The entire justice system has it out for you and you're just a victim of circumstance, is that right?"

Eric shrugged. "You finally see what I do, huh?"

I gaped at him for a moment then walked toward the exit where the guard stood. I couldn't stand being in the same room with him for another second.

"Jordana."

"What?" I said, stopping at the door. If he said one more thing about nothing being his fault, this was the last time I would be speaking to him.

"It's not—"

"Choose your words wisely, Eric. If I hear one more lie from you, I will *never* speak to you again."

I swore I heard his mouth clamp shut. So, he did care whether he saw me again. I left without a backward glance. Fists clenched. Jaw set. Backbone straight. Head held high. Why in the world had my mother even married him?

I drove out of the parking lot. Halfway to work I pulled over to the side of the road and bawled my eyes out. That was the first time I'd been honest with him and myself. Even though my dad was one of the crappiest, I held out hope for him to get his shit together. And every time he disappointed me hurt.

Every.

Damn.

Time.

Chapter Eight

Kane

I stayed on the bank of the drainage ditch, keeping out of sight until I saw Jordy's car drive off. From the position of the sun, I figured it was about eight or nine o'clock. I tested the lock of the slider, praying she'd left the door unlocked. The door glided over the track, and I slipped inside.

The room had been picked up. I opened the closet and found all the clothes that had been pulled out crammed inside. I'd promised to turn the room across the hall into one giant walk-in closet for her, but never got around to it. Jordy had a precise place for every item in this closet so it would all fit. Not today, though.

My stuff was always relegated to the closet in the room across the hall, except for what I could fit in the dresser. Okay, I had to stop reminiscing about what once was and get showered again. It wasn't as if I had all the time in the world here. I headed into the bathroom, took another shower, and brushed my teeth with a spare toothbrush I found in the drawer.

With a towel wrapped around my hips, I went to the spare bedroom across the hall and twisted the doorknob.

It was locked.

Okay. That was different.

Reaching up to the top of the door casing, I patted around for the emergency key tool.

Not there.

Okay, basement it is.

The wooden steps cooled my bare feet. If I thought the stairs were cold, the cement floor at the bottom was much worse. Jesus Christ, the floor was the temperature of ice. I shivered.

Along the far wall and stacked two-high and three-wide were boxes labeled "Kane" in thick black marker. Taped shut. I ripped the tape off the top box and pulled a pair of jeans off the top. The box next to it contained sets of sheets and a comforter. Why had she marked them as mine? I chuckled because, knowing Jordy, she wanted me to have something to put on a bed when I got out. The box underneath had my shoes. Five pairs, to be exact. Not sure why they needed their own box, though. I went through two more boxes before I found some boxers, socks, a T-shirt, and hoodie.

After throwing the clothes and sneakers on, I pivoted toward the stairs. My eye caught two more boxes sitting under the stairwell. One was labeled "M2M" and the other "Toys." What in the world could "M2M" mean? The box was taped, and it felt too nosy to open it. However, the "Toys" box was open. I peered inside, prepared for all my gaming equipment to be staring back at me, since I didn't remember seeing it in the house.

Not my gaming console. It was three-quarters filled with kids' toys. Little girl toys. Dolls. Pink plastic lawn mower that appeared to blow bubbles. Princess shoes. Wooden puzzles. That was all I could see. Why? Was she storing these toys for someone? Collecting for Toys for Tots?

Whatever the case, I needed to leave the house asap. Who knew if someone from the department would be back or whoever else was on the lookout for me. I headed upstairs.

Things I learned while in the ditch:

1.   I could hold my breath for longer than I thought.

2.   Jordy shouldn't have to suffer the consequences if I was caught before turning myself in.

3.   To avoid number 2, I had to turn myself in today.

4.   Jordy being fired or in jail because of me was worse than death.

Maybe I should've been pissed at her for having me arrested, yet I wasn't really. I understood why she'd taken Eric's side. She had always hoped her father would become the man he'd once had the potential to be.

Taking one last glance around the bedroom I had shared, and would never share again with Jordy, I left.

Next stop: FBI field office.

* * *

Jordana

I spent the rest of the morning and part of the afternoon all up in my own head. Well, when I wasn't making traffic stops. Fortunately, I had some paperwork back at the department to finish off the last few hours of my day.

Before I started on the worst part of the job, sitting behind a desk, I went to the break room for some coffee. I removed a Styrofoam cup from the plastic sleeve lying on the counter and picked up the pot from the warming plate. There wasn't enough left for even a quarter cup. Why didn't the last person to have a cup not make another pot? My shoulders dropped and I sighed heavily. *Fine. I'll do it.*

While the coffee brewed, I parked my butt in one of the chairs around the table. Out of the corner of my eye, I saw someone pass by the door, then come back and stand between the jambs.

Ryan Keith. A recently promoted detective and friend of Kane's. Or, more aptly put, ex-friend.

"How are you holding up?" Ryan asked with concern in his eyes.

"I'm okay. I'm not sure what you mean, though." My stomach soured. I knew why he asked.

"Oh, I guess you don't know."

"About Kane? I heard he escaped, some type of bus accident. The department was crawling all over my property." My face heated. Could he tell I'd harbored him last night?

'Yeah, there was a rollover involving the transport bus he was on."

I put my hand on the center of my chest. "Oh, my god, was anyone hurt?"

"Yeah. It was bad. Apparently, the bus was attacked. And Kane used the opportunity to run off, according to one of the guards who survived."

"I didn't realize it was so bad." I did realize. But did he realize Kane only ran because someone was shooting at him?

He nodded. "It was nasty, from what I heard. And—" Ryan cast his eyes away from mine—"there's a chance…Kane was injured—shot."

My eyes watered because all I could think about was what if Kane had drowned in the ditch. My heart squeezed. What if Ratchet was wrong? What if Willis had been lying? "Do you think he would try contacting me?"

"The thought occurred to me. Did you—I know this is none of my business, but did you ever tell him about Ava? You may want to have her spend a few days with your mom until he's apprehended. Just to be safe."

He wasn't wrong. That was none of his business. However, with Ryan Keith, his concern was always genuine, so I couldn't be mad at him. "Thanks, but she's already staying with them this week."

"I don't know if he'd be dumb enough to seek you out, but you never know."

"Even if he did, I don't think either of us would be in danger from him. He's not violent."

"No, not in the past, but prison is rough."

"I'm sorry, I realize prison has been known to

change a person's perspective, but this is Kane we're talking about." And he seemed the same to me last night. "You used to be friends."

His eyebrows rose. "That was before he broke the law. We are not friends. I don't trust the guy anymore. Do you?"

I sniffed, trying to keep myself from all-out bawling again. Ryan rose from his chair and stood closer to me. "Hey, I'm sorry."

"Why are you apologizing?"

"I upset you."

I shook myself. "No, you didn't."

"You're crying."

I wiped a tear from my cheek. Suddenly, my tears weren't because I was worried about Kane's safety and whereabouts. "I never told him about Ava," I gushed. "Am I a bad person?"

"No. You were protecting yourself and her."

Was I, or was I just being selfish? I didn't want to feel obligated to step one foot into that prison again. He had the right to know he had a daughter. His parents had the right to know they had a grandchild. Kane was their only child. Their only chance for a grandbaby. "His parents don't even know they have a granddaughter. And they were always good to me."

Ryan put his arm around my shoulders. He didn't say anything more, and who could blame him? "I gotta get to work," I said, pulling away.

"Emily and I are here for you if you need to talk."

I smiled tightly. "Thanks."

* * *

As I was gathering my purse to leave for the day, my desk phone rang. "This is Officer Brooklyn," I answered.

The man on the other end of the call cleared his throat. "Uh, yeah, this is Jonathan Banks, the warden down at—"

"I know who you are. How can I help you?"

"This is about Eric Brooklyn."

I rubbed my forehead. "Is he all right?"

"He's at Westville General in the ICU."

"What happened? Did he have a heart attack?" I asked because he chained smoked when he wasn't behind bars.

"No, ma'am. He was attacked earlier today by another inmate. He's expected to recover but he's in bad shape. I thought you'd want to know."

"Thanks. Do you know why—what the altercation was about?"

"Your father keeps to himself. So, who knows? The other prisoner was new to the facility."

"Thank you for letting me know."

"You're welcome. You can visit him in the hospital if you want."

"It's that bad, huh?"

The warden paused for a few moments.

"Are you still there?"

He sighed. "Yeah. The doctors said he'll pull through."

I sighed, relieved he at least wasn't dying. "Okay, thank you for letting me know."

I had met the warden a few times before, so the call was a professional courtesy.

The warden grumbled something I assumed was

"yeah" and "goodbye." I hung up the phone and grabbed my purse from the desk drawer.

I tossed my Vera Bradley bag on the front passenger seat as I got behind the wheel of my car. I managed to catch every damn light en route to the hospital. As I pulled into the circular ER drive, a security guard waved me onto the parking lot.

Getting out of the car, I took out my cell and dialed my mom. She picked up on the third ring. "Did you hear?" I blurted before she said hello.

"Jordana?"

"Did you hear about Eric?"

"What about your dad?"

I walked quickly toward the automatic double doors. "He's in the hospital. He was attacked by another inmate."

"Uh, no, I didn't. Is he okay?"

"Yeah, but from what the warden said he's in pretty bad shape."

The ER doors slid open, and I went to the triage station. A nurse smiled up at me expectantly. "Eric Brooklyn? I'm his daughter." It dawned on me how, this morning, I wasn't liking him much, and now I was panicked that our last conversation had not ended well, and I might *really* never speak to him again.

I swore under my breath. Okay, Eric ruined my relationship. On purpose. However, I needed to know who attacked my father and why. And was the beating in any way connected to the ambush on Kane's bus?

The nurse typed something into the computer, her attention focused on the screen. "Ah, yes, here he is.

He's in the ICU. You can ask the nurses' station up there what room he's in. Do you know how to get there?"

I shook my head as my mom babbled through the phone in my ear.

"Take the elevators around the corner to the fifth floor."

"Thanks."

"Who are you talking to?" my mom asked.

"A nurse."

"Oh, you're at the hospital now?"

"Yeah. I'm heading to the ICU. I'll probably lose you in the elevator. How's Ava?"

"She's fine. Do you want to say hello? She's right next to me."

"No, wait—" There was some rustling on the other end.

"Hi, Mommy."

"Hey, sweetheart. Are you having fun with Grandma and Pop-pop?"

"Uh-huh."

I pushed the "UP" button for the elevator. "What did you do today?"

"We went to the park!" Ava spoke with such enthusiasm that you would have thought she went to Disneyland instead of a parcel of land with a few swing sets.

"Awesome! Did you go on the swings?"

"Uh-huh, and we had a picnic."

"That sounds like fun." I wished I had gone with them. My day was anything but a picnic. And it wasn't even over yet.

"It was fun!"

"Listen, Ava, Mommy's got to go. I love you. Can you put Grand—"

"I love you, too. Bye, Mommy." There was some shuffling and the connection ended.

The elevator doors slid open. Two people dressed in scrubs exited, leaving me alone for the ride to the ICU floor. A nurse at the nurses' station directed me to room 510. For some stupid reason, this made me think of Kane. He'd gotten ten years. *Ten years*. I had to keep reminding myself of that. Out after three and a half, because his prison transport bus was ambushed. When the Feds caught up to him, who knew how much more time they would tack onto his sentence. God, I wished I could get Ava, find Kane, and go someplace without extradition.

But what was I thinking? My dad was severely beaten, I'd miss my parents, Ava would miss my parents, and there was an entire slew of other reasons why the idea was preposterous.

The door to room 510 was propped open and an officer was parked on a chair in the hallway. "Eric is my father," I said, even though the man hadn't asked. He glanced at my police uniform and nametag.

"J. Brooklyn," he said.

"Yes. The J's for Jordana." Again, he hadn't asked.

He nodded. "Go ahead, knock yourself out."

"Do you know anything about what happened?"

"Not much."

"Who attacked him?"

He shrugged.

Thank you, you've been most unhelpful.

I moved past him into the room. My father lay on

the bed with wires hanging off him and an oxygen tube stuck in his nose. I approached the bed on wobbly legs. Bruises marred his face and the swelling around his eyes made him almost unrecognizable. His eyes were closed, or more likely swollen shut.

A nurse came into the room. She smiled warmly. "I heard he had a visitor."

"Yeah, um, is he—why is he on oxygen?"

"His levels were low. But don't worry, he's already showing signs of improvement."

"Was he unconscious when he was brought in?"

"In and out from what I heard. He has a bad concussion."

I nodded. "Okay. Is that why he is in the ICU?" She gave me a funny look and shrugged. "Ah, never mind. It must be because this is a more secure and less occupied floor."

She smiled. "Yeah. I didn't want to say that."

I sighed. "It is what it is. I know who he is and the why of it."

"A patient is a patient to me, regardless if they are the President of the United States or a—"

"Convict?"

"I want him to get better, no matter who he is or what he has done."

"Oh, yeah, I wasn't trying to imply that you wouldn't treat him the same as everyone else."

"I wanted you to know that he will receive the best care possible here." She checked his temperature and took a reading from his blood pressure cuff.

"Is his doctor around? I'd like to speak to them, if possible."

"I'll have her paged. She should still be here."

"When do you think he'll be released?"

"Not sure. Doctor Bingham can answer your questions." The nurse finished typing on a tablet and left the room.

"Eric," I said, leaning over the bedrail. His eyes moved beneath the lids. I waited for a few seconds to see if he would open them. "It's me. Your daughter. Guess you're not talking."

There was a first for everything. He always had something to say. I wouldn't use the word clever to describe him, but he always seemed to have a ready response to anything. The night he told me Kane was involved in a bank heist, he'd said I should be more worried about what my fiancé was up to than about him. Eric accused me of projecting my emotional insecurities onto him. I accused him of spending the money Kane and I had given him on drugs instead of his rent. Little did I know, he'd gambled the money and owed some bad people a lot of cash. Although, I'd caught him using in my bathroom that night, too. I'd found residue on the counter after he'd been in there for twenty minutes. And he never flushed the toilet or ran any water.

I looked him over, making my own assessment of his injuries. His arm was in a splint. There were defensive wounds on his other arm. "Who did this to you? And why?" If I had to guess, he'd been running his mouth about the bank heist or pissing off the wrong inmate. My father did have a big mouth. The gift of gab. Or, more like the curse of a big fat mouth. Liar mouth. How could I have been so stupid? So insecure to believe his lies about…about everything, my whole life?

My willingness to overlook my father's faults and history in order to gain his love and acceptance was so strong, it was sickening. Never had he told me he was proud of me, but Kane told me all the time.

Of all the times Eric disappointed me when I was growing up, I remembered one specifically, when I was eight, the most:

The Christmas tree lights twinkled. The house smelled of the sugar cookies my mom and I had baked and decorated for Santa. I lay on the floor in front of the tree, drawing pictures. Dad was coming over tonight, too. I set aside three of the cookies so we could frost them together. The gift I made for him at school sat under the tree: an ornament with my school picture in it.

"That's a really nice drawing," Mom said as she sat next to me on the floor. "Tell me about it."

"Well," I said, pointing to the paper I'd drawn our family on. "This is me, Daddy, you, and over here is Robert."

Her brow creased. "Why is Robert so far away from us?"

I shrugged. "He's not my real dad."

"True, but your stepdad is still part of this family."

"I know." My stomach flip-flopped. I liked Robert. He took care of me and my mom and he was out making the streets of Westville safe for everyone. "When will daddy get here?"

She checked her watch. "Should be soon. He's taking you out for Christmas Eve dinner at the Chinese restaurant you like.

"He is?" I jumped up.

"Yes. So why don't you put your drawing stuff away and wash your hands and put on your pretty new dress before he gets here?"

I ran to the bathroom, excited to see my dad and wear the dress I'd gotten that day. It was red plaid with a black velvet ribbon around the waist that tied in a bow. My shoes even had little bows on them.

On my way back to the living room, the phone rang in the kitchen. My heart skipped and I stopped in the hallway to listen.

"Hello," Mom said. She sighed. "What is it this time, Eric?"

I squeezed my eyes shut. Dad was calling to cancel. I just knew it. "No, you can't talk to her. What are you going to say anyway...? I'll tell her. Jordy's going to be very disappointed..."

I ran to my bedroom and threw myself on the bed and cried. Mom knocked on the door. "Jordy?"

"He's not coming, is he?"

"I'm sorry, sweetheart."

I hated that she always felt she needed to apologize for him. It was as if she blamed herself for his actions. "Just once, I'd like an apology from you," I said to my dad's prone form.

The officer stationed at the door greeted someone, who responded in kind. I glanced over my shoulder at a middle-aged woman in scrubs and a lab coat. "Hi," I said.

She smiled. "You must be his daughter. I was told you were visiting. I'm Dr. Bingham."

"Yeah, I'm Jordana. Do you think he'll wake up

soon? I'd like to talk to him."

"He should. He's only sleeping." She scanned the iPad in her hands. "His oxygen levels are improving. If that continues, we'll take him off the oxygen tomorrow and he'll be released in a couple days."

"Thanks." I wanted to shake him. "Would I be the worst daughter in the world if I smacked him awake?"

Her forehead crinkled and she smirked. "I cannot condone that."

"What?"

"You asked if you would be the worst daughter if you smacked—"

"I said that out loud, huh?"

"Is there a number I can add to his file so I can contact you if necessary?"

I gave her my cell number. "Did he say anything when he came in?" Like whom did this to him?

"Not that I recall. He was pretty out of it."

I nodded. A few minutes later, the doctor left me alone with him, besides the other officer who looked like he was playing a game on his cell. Head down. Hunched over. Elbows on his knees.

God, I wanted to scream at Eric for ruining my life in more ways than one. He was the reason for my insecurities. Why my only response was to rat out Kane instead of talking to him. I always expected the men in my life to disappoint me. It was even why I also kept Robert at a distance. I couldn't trust my own father, so why would any other man be any different?

Kane was.

Robert was.

Had I realized the truth, maybe I would have made another choice. I could have tried to convince Kane to go to the FBI instead of committing a felony.

Now, he was a fugitive with next to no future, and I was a broken-hearted single mother pining for my ex-fiancé.

Chapter Nine

Jordana

All I wanted to do was find Kane and hug him. It sucked that he was the only one to whom I looked for comfort, even after over three years apart. He was my home and security blanket. Where had he gone after leaving the house? Would I ever see him again?

I raced to the department after leaving the hospital, hoping I could catch Ryan before he went home. He wasn't at his desk when I arrived. Dammit. His car was still in the lot though. Searching the station, I came up emptyhanded. Where could he be? Did I just miss—

Ryan laughed down the hall. I followed the sound to the break room. He stepped around the corner, chuckling with his old partner, Nate. I speed-walked toward him. "Ryan!" I shouted because, screw it, he was the only one I trusted with what I was about to confess, and he was nearly out the door.

He pivoted and waited for me. I was out of breath

and sweaty. His brow furrowed. "Are you okay?"

"Can I talk to you in private?" Really, I meant in private and in confidence.

"Sure, are you okay?"

"I'm fine." I huffed.

"For the record, I don't believe you. What's going on?"

"Not here. It isn't something I want to talk about out in the open."

"I already know about your dad. Is that what this is about?"

"It's not. Well, not entirely. Please, can we talk in my car?"

"All right. After you." We walked mutely to my car, side by side. Once we were in with the doors closed and the AC cranked, he turned to me. "I hear your dad's going to recover."

"He's fine." Probably fake-sleeping at the hospital so he didn't have to talk to me. I took a deep breath. "I, uh, think I know why he was attacked."

"Things like that happen in prison all the time."

"I know, but not to Eric. He's been in and out of prison I don't know how many times and, as far as I know, this has never happened to him before. He's passive, so why would anyone pick on some middle-aged man who minds his own business, especially in a low security prison?"

"What do you think happened, then?"

I stared straight ahead out the front windshield. "I think this has to do with Kane."

His eyebrows rose. "In what way?"

"Do you know how I knew about the bank heist?"

"Yeah, you suspected Kane was involved in

something and you followed him—"

"Eric told me. That's the only reason I knew anything."

"Okay. Then my question is: how did he know? You never mentioned that Eric tipped you off."

"That's because I didn't want to involve him. You know he has problems. I made a mistake not saying anything. I thought my father heard about it from someone he knows. He knows...*people*." Scum of the earth people, but people, nonetheless.

"He heard about it from Kane?"

"Yeah, but he lied. He knew a lot more than he admitted to me. He got into some trouble gambling and wound up owing a lot of money to some...people. Anyway, he went to Kane for help. And Kane being Kane, he thought he could talk to these people. Reason with them. Except Eric was in deep shit and they threatened his life, Eric's, and mine. So he made a deal with them to make my father's debt go away."

Ryan pinched the bridge of his nose. "The deal was to drive the getaway car."

"Yes. To protect me," I answered him even though it was a statement rather than a question.

"Shit, Brooklyn. How do you know all this? Do I even want to know?"

I swallowed hard. "No."

"Where is he?"

I gaped at Ryan. If I tried denying Kane had come to see me, the detective would know I lied. "I don't know."

"Do I need to remind you that you're a cop? Where is he? Where is Kane?"

"I don't know where he went."

"But you saw him?"

I nodded.

"Fuck. This isn't good." Now Ryan was staring out the windshield like me.

"I know. But I didn't invite him over. He showed up on my doorstep in the middle of the night. I couldn't—"

"You should have—"

"I couldn't turn him in. I have enough guilt on my conscience."

"Guilt about what?"

"Ava. Betraying him instead of confronting him, and not helping him figure out what to do before he resorted to robbing a bank." Despite that Kane only drove the getaway, he was still guilty of the entire crime.

"Why didn't you?"

"I don't know. Daddy issues."

Ryan chuckled without humor. "Well, I suppose I'd be pretty messed up, too, had my dad been in and out of prison instead of Chief of Police."

"Thanks." I flopped my head against the seat. "I know my dad is a piece of shit."

"Sorry, I didn't mean how that sounded."

"It's okay. You're not wrong."

"I have to contact the FBI. Can you think of anything that might help Kane? As much as I hate that he did this, we were once friends. And if he was coerced into doing this to protect you..." He ran a hand down the side of his face.

"He mentioned something about there being more players in the game. Someone else was calling the shots. I think Eric was blabbing to another inmate about the organization behind the robbery and word got out."

"Good possibility. Do you think he could identify them?"

"Yes." *God, I hope.* "The attack on the prison transport was an assassination attempt. That's why Kane ran."

"Then your father was attacked."

"Uh-huh. Could be a coincidence, but I doubt it. Someone was trying to shut him up."

"Most likely. You know, I'm gonna—fuck—let me make a call to the FBI agent in charge of the investigation and I'll get back to you." He opened the door.

"Ryan. Ava can't lose me. She's already down one parent."

"Then let's hope Kane has more information than he provided in his testimony."

* * *

Kane

All right, so I'd been prepared to turn myself in after leaving the house, but I wasn't ready to die just yet. I situated a baseball cap on my head, avoiding the surveillance cameras in the convenience store, and ducked outside. I'd been to this store many times in the past. However, the guy behind the counter was someone I didn't recognize. With the hat and sunglasses I'd also swiped, hopefully I could elude capture for a few days until I sorted this mess out. I had little doubt Eric was squealing in prison about the men who'd planned the bank heist. Except I was the only one of us that committed the crime who had seen the big boss man.

Unfortunately, I never learned his real name, only his alias. The Duke. Fan of John Wayne, was he?

I walked a few miles to a small tavern outside of town known as a watering hole for bikers. I'd never set one foot in the place, but it seemed like a seedy enough dive I could get lost in for a while.

As I'd imagined, the dimly lit joint hosted a small crew of bikers and their babes, the kind who were inked up with skulls, flames, eagles, and "Ride to Live" tattoos. I parked my ass on a stool at the bar. A bartender poured beer from a tap and set the glass in front of an elderly man.

Above the bar, a flatscreen was on with the volume on mute so subtitles ran across the bottom. The program ended and the news came on. A couple of the bikers laughed somewhere behind me. I peeked over my shoulder. They weren't paying any attention to me. Thank god. One of them kind of looked familiar, though.

"What can I get you?" the bartender asked, surprising me. I faced forward. He was standing in front of me with his hands on the bar top. He wore a red plaid shirt with the sleeves rolled up, revealing a faded prison tattoo. His long, gray-and-black peppered hair was pulled back in a pony and he had the deep lines of a heavy smoker around his mouth and eyes.

I still had the fifty from the trucker. "Beer."

"Bottle or tap? Bud, Coors...I got Corona...?"

"Bud on tap if you got it." He grabbed a glass and dispensed the amber liquid, filling it to the top. Foam dribbled down the side. "Thanks," I said as he placed the beer on the bar.

"You're welcome. Just flag me when you need a refill."

How did he know I needed the beers to keep coming? Although, getting drunk shouldn't be anywhere near what I needed. While I nursed my beer, I glanced at the TV. My face flashed on the screen. Fuck. I read the closed captioning. *Police and the local FBI are on a manhunt for the escaped prisoner, Kane Adler. If you see this man, authorities are warning people not to approach him as he may be armed. Instead call 9-1-1.*

I wasn't armed.

The bartender leaned against the counter with his arms folded across his chest. He shrugged then changed the channel with a remote.

I sipped my beer, wondering if the guy recognized me from my unfortunate television debut. He came over and refilled my glass. I kept my head down.

A chair behind me scraped against the floor as someone pushed away from the table. The biker I thought I recognized came and leaned against the bar next to me. Oh, great, this was what I needed right now. "I know you," he said.

"I don't think you do," I said into my beer.

"Yeah, I do." He leaned into my personal space. His alcohol breath pelted my face. Clearly this shit-for-brains had never done any hard time.

"No, you don't, so go back to your table and mind your own business." I shook my head. Man, this fidiot didn't know how low my blood sugar was. I wanted to punch him. But I didn't need the bartender calling the police. Fuck me.

"I *said* I know you." He jabbed my shoulder with three fingers, twisting my upper body away from the bar top.

My hands curled into fists. "Back. The. Fuck. Up."

"And if I don't?"

I ground my molars. *Dear god, don't make me do this.* "What's with you, man?" Seriously, I was minding my own fucking business and this dude— come *on,* man.

"I don't like you."

"I don't know why, and I don't care." I sipped my beer even though this jerk was staring down at me. I refused to look at him.

"You'll care when I put my fist through your face."

Through my face. How was that going to work? "Not sure I even know what that means. You sound like an idiot."

The bartender glanced over for the first time and snorted.

"What did you call me?" Fidiot said.

My response should've been to throw a few bucks on the bar and leave the establishment. However, that wasn't what happened. "I called you an idiot."

"All right," the bartender said. "Jacob Barrett, I told you to quick picking fights in my bar."

The fidiot recoiled like the bartender was a snake and he'd lashed out at him with his fangs. "But this guy—"

"I don't wanna hear it. Go sit down or I'll remove you permanently."

Jacob sneered at me and slinked off. Obviously, this bar must've been his favorite place for him to obey the bartender so readily.

"Thanks," I said to the bartender.

"You hungry?"

I couldn't remember the last time I ate. After I left our—Jordy's—house and decided not to turn myself in yet, I'd wandered the streets with no direction in mind. "I could eat." The bartender handed me a menu printed on a thick wrinkled piece of 8 1/2 x 11. I scanned the paper and ordered a bar burger and fries.

After returning from the kitchen, the bartender sat on a stool behind the bar near me. "What's your name?" I asked him.

"Chet."

"Is this your bar?"

"Yeah. Inherited from my ol' man a few years back. It's not much but it keeps a roof over my head and food on the table. Keeps me out of trouble."

"Why's that?"

"I'm a responsible business owner now." He winked. "Naw. It's more than that. My ol' man worked his ass off running the place. I figured I owe it to him to keep the place open for what I put him through growing up."

"How long ago did he pass?"

"Fifteen years. What about you, your folks still around?"

"Yeah." And fuck, what I had put my parents through. My mom visited me religiously every week for the first two years. Then once a month for a while, until eventually she stopped coming altogether. I didn't blame her. She would get teary eyed every time she said goodbye. There wasn't anything I could say to console her. No matter the reason I chose the path I followed, I was stuck in prison until I turned thirty-eight.

"You're lucky to have them still around."

I snort-chuckled quietly. "I don't think the feeling's mutual."

"You seem all right to me."

"Because you don't know me."

"I know more than you think, kid." The cook dinged a bell. Chet grabbed my food from the back and served me the plate. Without asking, he got me a glass of ice water.

I took a long sip. *Ahhh.* "Thanks."

Chet sat back down on his stool.

I ate my burger. Drank another beer. We chatted off and on for a few hours about nothing in particular until it was getting dark outside, and the place had cleared out. "What's my tab?" I asked Chet.

"You don't owe me anything."

I shook my head. "No, I couldn't take advantage of your hospitality."

He waved me off. "You know why I never asked for your name?"

"I can guess. Thanks, by the way, for that and the food."

"You're welcome, Officer Adler. You arrested my son, Jacob."

Ah, that was how I knew the fidiot. I should have known. "Then shouldn't you be pissed at me, and not serving me free dinner and drinks?"

He shook his head. "He deserved it. His ex-wife was like a daughter to me. I hated what was going on and knew it wouldn't stop until something was done."

I smiled as relief washed over me. "I noticed your tat. Where'd you do your time?"

"San Quentin."

"Rough place. I imagine the stories are all true."

He half-smiled. "And then some. You have anywhere to sleep tonight?"

I shrugged.

"Thought so. I have an office back behind the bar with a comfortable couch with your name on it if you want. One night only."

I shouldn't trust anybody right now. For all I knew, he planned on calling the police as soon as I fell asleep. Or he'd lock me in his office and then contact the FBI. "Fuck it, sure. But why are you helping me if you know who I am?"

"I may have had it bad in The Arena, but nothing like you ex-cops have in prison."

"It's not so bad if you don't mind getting a daily beat down."

Chet laughed. "I bet you're twice the size you were when you went in."

I pumped my fists like I was lifting weights. "It helped." But bigger muscles only meant bigger guys would pick fights with me.

Chet unlocked the office, and I went inside. He didn't follow. Yep, just as I thought, he trapped me. I shouldn't've been so stup—

"Can I ask you something? You don't have to answer— but what made you turn to crime? Was it the lure of the quick score or something else?"

I sat on the couch. "Something else."

He nodded. "Do you regret it?"

"Only that I got caught."

"Must have been a big something else for that to be your only regret."

"It was."

"It's Sunday night, so I'm closing early. I'll be here tomorrow afternoon for a liquor delivery."

"Thank you. I won't forget what you've done here."

Chet nodded then left, leaving the office door open, perhaps so that I wouldn't feel caged in.

Honestly, I didn't expect I'd be able to fall asleep, but as I stretched out on the couch, my eyelids became too heavy to keep open.

There was no telling how long I'd been asleep when I woke up. Man, my mouth was dry.

I sat up and put my feet on the floor. Stretched. "What time is it?" I mumbled to myself. There wasn't a clock in the office, so I got up and flipped open the laptop on the desk. According to the screen, it was 4:10 AM.

Fuck. I rubbed the back of my neck. It was too early to be awake, but my mouth was dry. So, I lurched out of the back office to the bar for a glass of water. Behind the bar, I found a glass and poured myself some water from the faucet.

I stood at the sink, gulping it down. After the glass was empty, I refilled it and—

I heard a noise behind me and spun around. I hadn't heard anyone break in. Had someone else been there with me overnight?

Before me stood Jacob Barrett, plus a friend.

Jesus Christ. Just when I thought I'd caught a break for a damn minute. I set my glass down. "Whadda you want?"

"To settle this."

"We have nothing to settle. Go home."

"See, I was almost convinced that I mistook you for someone else until I saw the news when I got home."

"You watch the news? Good for you. Do you also read?" Barrett's friend cracked his knuckles. I shook my head. Did he think that made him seem tougher? "You know what they say about people who crack their knuckles, don't you?"

"Wives' tale," the knuckle cracker said. "Doesn't give you arthritis."

"You're right, it doesn't. Means you gotta small dick." Yes, I was asking for a beating, but at this point, it was inevitable. I wanted to get the smackdown over with. Hey, maybe they'd knock me out and I'd get in a longer nap.

Barrett chuckled without humor. "The way I see it, you're in no position to make jokes."

"I'm not? Whatever score you think you have to *settle* with me is in the past. And—" I raised my index finger—"if my memory serves me well, and I think it does, I arrested you about seven years ago for domestic violence. After a fair trial, you only served eighteen months on a five-year sentence. The way I see it, we have nothing to settle. You got off easy."

"My wife left me."

"How is that my fault? You were beating the shit out of her. Do you blame her?"

"I blame you."

I snorted. "The fuck is with you?" I glanced at his friend, who nodded like he actually believed I was to blame. Barrett's wife was the one who'd called the police and pressed charges. The last I'd heard was she moved far away from here after the trial. And apparently stayed away. "Oh, I get it, so now you think you can kick my ass and get away with it because I won't call the police. You know if you really wanted to fuck me over, you could've just called them and saved yourself the hassle of coming down here."

"I happen to like this place. Brings back a lot of memories for me."

"Good for you. Does your father know you're here? Do I have to call him and have him drag you out of here by the ear?"

"Shut up!"

Jacob's friend snorted.

"You shut up, too."

All right. I wasn't going to be talking my way out of this. The man wanted a fight. Barrett I could handle, but with the two of them, this fight probably wasn't going to end in my favor. I walked around to their side of the bar. "I'm ready when you are."

Barrett lunged at me, slamming me up against the bar. His right fist came at my head. I ducked and threw a punch, hitting him in the cheek. He stumbled back and that was the last thing I remembered. I'd lost track of Barrett's friend when he hit me on the head with something hard.

Did I hear glass break?

Chapter Ten

Kane

I heard water running. *Where am I?* I lifted my head off the cold floor and winced. My head throbbed. Well, I wasn't in the hospital or on a concrete prison floor, so that was something. A large pair of feet covered in black boots appeared in my line of sight. The person squatted next to me. "It's a good thing we're closed on Mondays," Chet said.

"My head hurts." I moaned, gathering the strength to sit up. Finally, I managed to get my torso off the floor.

He handed me a small wet towel. "For your head."

"Thanks."

"Someone clocked you one, I see," Chet said, rising to his full height.

"Your son's an asshole." I dabbed at the back of my head.

Chet laughed. "I'd like to blame his mother for how he turned out, but I was the same way when I was his age. Younger, even. Experience taught me a better way to be."

"Would this experience have anything to do with prison?"

"I'd be lying if I said no. Here." Chet offered me his hand for a boost off the floor. I grabbed it and he pulled me to my feet. A wave of the woozies washed over me and I used the bar to keep from falling. The tsunami passed after a few seconds, allowing me to stand without assistance.

"If you called the police, can you tell me now so I can get a head start? Better yet, can you take me to the FBI field office?"

"You're giving up?"

"I've given it a lot of thought. So far this week, I've been in a bus accident, shot at, nearly drowned in shit, and now bashed over the head. I'm about done."

"What will happen to you when you turn yourself in?" Chet sat on one of the bar stools.

"I'll likely be murdered by whoever ordered the attack on the prison bus. I don't know what the news said about the accident, but it was a hit."

"The news said there was evidence of gunfire."

I nodded. "I'm not armed, by the way, and never was. I fled the scene because I didn't feel like dying."

"But you do now?"

I shrugged. "I don't want anyone to get hurt because of me."

Chet nodded. "You know, when you first walked into my bar, I recognized you as the cop who arrested my son. Not as a fugitive. You asked if I was pissed and my answer is still the same. No. You were right to arrest him. I'm the one who called the police that night."

"I thought she did."

"That's what she said." We both chuckled. "I dialed the phone, she talked. Ripped the phone right out of my hand. I thought she was going to hang up, but—"

"She surprised you."

"Yeah. I still would've called."

"I'm not going to ask why because I think I can guess."

"Good, because I'm not going to tell you. I'm helping you out because you helped Lucy, Jacob's wife. You went out of your way to follow up with her and make sure she was doing okay. I wanted to thank you somehow for going the extra. He may be my son but that doesn't mean I love everything he does." He got off the stool and clapped his hands. "Let's get some food into you and I'll drive you wherever you wanna go."

Chet made the best omelet I'd ever tasted while I cleaned my latest head wound. Or maybe I was just incredibly hungry. We left the bar at four in the afternoon and drove to the FBI field office.

"Can you drive around the block?" I asked when we approached the building where the FBI offices were located.

"Second thoughts?"

"No, just need a min—what the fuck?" When we passed the building, Morrison was walking out of the building. I watched the guard until we turned the corner out of sight.

"What is it?"

"I just saw one of the prison guards that was on the bus with me. I thought he was dying at the scene, but he didn't look injured at all."

"Maybe it wasn't him?"

"It was him."

Fuuuck.

"Still want me to drop you here?"

"No. I have somewhere else to be now."

* * *

Jordana

I didn't remember the drive home from work. And getting out of the car seemed like too much work. I sat in the garage with the engine off, trying not to puke. Did I just blow up my life? What if Ryan told the FBI agent that I had abetted a fugitive? What if he was only pretending to believe Kane's theory? My gut churned. What had I done?

A sob bubbled up from my throat. Oh, God, Ava...Kane. I gagged. Once. Twice. I bolted from my car and ran for the garbage can in the garage. After the evac of everything I ate that day, I was shaking.

I entered the house and headed for the bathroom and brushed my teeth. *That's odd.* I didn't remember leaving the light on that morning.

"Don't freak out." Someone appeared behind me in the mirror.

"Uh!" I went for the gun at my hip and spun.

Kane waved his hands. "Hey, it's just me. It's just me. Please don't shoot."

I relaxed and dropped my hand, although my heart

pounded. "You scared the shit out of me."

'I'm sorry."

I threw my arms around him and rested my head on his chest. "What happened to you last night?"

"Long story. Listen, Jordy, I shouldn't've left you alone. I saw one of the guards from the bus accident coming out of the FBI office. It's not safe for you here."

Or for Ava, I tacked on in my mind.

Swallowing hard, I put some inches between us so I could look at his face. "Why were you at the FBI office? Were you going to turn yourself in?"

"I was until I saw Morrison. I had to make sure you were safe."

"You think he's going to come here?"

"I do, so let's get you someplace safe." The until-I'm-back-in-prison was implied.

"Eric was attacked."

"Fuck. Even more reason we need to get you out of here now."

"How long ago did you see Morrison?"

The doorbell rang.

"Are you expecting company?" Kane asked.

"No." I moved past him, heading for the front door. He followed right behind me. "See who it is first before you—"

"Yeah, on it." I glanced through the peephole. "It's Ryan Keith."

"Lyin' Ryan?"

"He's changed. He's also a detective now. You should probably hide."

A gun fired. The sidelight glass shattered. "Get down!" Kane shouted. Another round rang out...*POP!* Kane opened the front door and yanked Ryan inside. They fell to the floor. "Stay down. Head for the garage!"

"No shit, Adler," Ryan barked.

POP!

POP!

We crawled to the garage door through the kitchen.

"What the fuck, Kane?" Ryan said, once we were all in the garage.

"You're welcome."

"If you're looking for a thank-you from me, you're not getting one. Who the fuck is shooting at us?"

Kane threw his hands up in exasperation. "Oh, I don't know, the people who attacked the prison bus I was on. Morrison."

Ryan and Kane glared at each other.

"Is that where the nasty gash on your head came from?"

"I didn't do it to myself."

"If someone is after you, why would you come here and endanger Jordana and your—?"

"Stop, you guys," I said, standing between them. Although Ryan knew Kane didn't know about his daughter, secrets could spill in heated situations.

A loud noise caught everyone's attention. We snapped our heads in the direction of the door leading into the kitchen. The shooters were in the house knocking stuff over. Banging doors. Shouting at each other.

Fortunately, I grabbed my car keys from the counter. I motioned for Kane and Ryan to get in the car. Thankfully, neither decided to play the hero by marching back into the house.

Once the garage door lifted enough for my car to pull through, I backed out, K-turned onto the street, and sped away from the house. Ryan called the home invasion into dispatch.

"Drop me around the corner," Ryan said.

"Don't do anything stupid," Kane said.

"I'm not you. I'm waiting for backup." When we made it around the block, Ryan got out of the car and took a key off his keyring and handed it to me through the window. "That's to the apartment in the Soar Xtreme hangar at Falcon Airport. It's safe and private. Do yourselves a favor and stay put. I'll be in touch."

Chapter Eleven

Kane

It was too bad I didn't know how to fly a plane. I entertained the idea of escaping with Jordy to someplace without extradition. A country we could get lost in, change our names, and live happily ever after.

That could totally happen, couldn't it?

She parked the car a half mile from the airport, and we walked the rest of the way in the dark. I was still floating on the escape fantasy when reality slammed into me with the force of a semi-truck. Jordy sat on the bed inside the hangar apartment, with her face in her hands.

What was I doing? Being murdered and turned into roadkill would've been less painful than watching the woman I loved suffer because of me.

"Do you think this place has anything to eat?" *Oh, terrific, good one.* I asked her about food instead of telling her what was really on my mind. I loved her and would be surrendering myself to Ryan the next time we saw him.

I gave her a tissue from the box on the bedside stand. She didn't wipe her tears though, merely folded it over and over on her thigh.

I scrubbed my face with my palms. "I'm so sorry. I shouldn't have involved you."

"I chose to open the door."

"I shouldn't have put you in that position." I started pacing.

She shrugged. "The door is open now so—"

"So, I should be the one to close it. I'm surrendering myself to Ryan."

"There may be a chance we can turn this around. You said there are more players involved in the bank robbery—if you know who they are, then why not tell the FBI?"

"It's a little late for that, don't you think?" I stopped and stood in front of her.

"If these people want you and Eric dead, then they are worried you know who they are. And I'm not stupid. You do know."

I began pacing again. "I only know what the guy calling the shots looks like. I never got a real name."

"Could you identify him if you saw him again?"

"Yeah. But it's difficult to find someone who knows how not to get caught."

"Can you please stop pacing? You're going to carve a rut in the floor." Jordy got off the bed and I took the spot she vacated.

She removed her service belt and laid it on the kitchenette table.

"Where's your gun?" I asked.

"At the department. I don't bring it home with me." She said this as if it were her usual routine and I was crazy for asking.

"Since when?"

"A lot of things have changed since you last saw me."

"Yesterday?"

She shook her head. "No, Kane. Since you went to prison."

"What other things?"

"Paint. Furniture. How I spend my nights and days off."

My chest tightened. Sure, I had no right to be jealous, yet this fact didn't stop the emotion from happening, though. "I thought you said you weren't seeing anyone?"

"I'm not."

"What do you spend your time off doing?"

"Don't worry, I'm not having sex," she said in a *not-that-it's-any-of-your-business* tone.

I smiled sheepishly. "Sorry. I have no right to control what you do with your time or who you see."

"Did you ever?"

"You know what I mean."

"Yeah...I know," she said quietly.

"So, have you dated at all?" Although I hated the idea of her having a romantic relationship with someone else, I didn't want her to spend her life alone. She deserved happiness. She shook her head. "Not even one date?"

Her face flushed. "A few dates a year ago. I don't have a lot of spare time to myself *to* date."

How could this be? I couldn't help feeling

responsible. "Please tell me I didn't scare you off getting involved with other men."

She smirked. "Don't flatter yourself. I honestly don't have time."

"Why?" I asked. "You couldn't carve out a little time to get busy?"

She rolled her eyes. "Kane. Really? Just drop it."

"All right, I will. But *no* action?" God, I wanted to lighten the mood so desperately, I was willing to joke about her having sex with another man. Okay, yes, I had a problem with it, but I'd once thought I'd be spending the rest of my life with her.

Jordy smiled. "Fine, I had sex once." She blushed. "But I'm not telling you with whom, so don't even ask."

"Willis?" I grinned.

She snorted. "Willis? No. Why would you think that? And besides, I just told you not to ask."

"But I wanna know."

"I can see that. Too bad."

"Can't you tell me anything? Who was better?"

Her eyes widened. "Are you serious? Why do you want to know that?"

"Uh, because." I laughed even though I really did want to know, and I had no idea why it mattered other than the fact that I was jealous. Not crazy, I-want-to-kick-this-other-guy's-ass jealous, but jealous.

"Don't be ridiculous. I'm not telling you anything."

I hung my head then raised my eyes and peeked at her. "So, he is better in the sack."

Jordy shook her head. "I didn't say *that*."

"Good." I grinned and puffed my chest.

"Oh, my god. You're so silly." She untucked and unbuttoned her uniform shirt.

"Am I going to get a striptease?"

"Maybe." She gave me a sideways glance and shrugged out of her shirt. "No. I want to get this vest off."

"Need some help? The Velcro on a Kevlar vest can be tricky."

"I think I can handle it." She pulled at the side Velcro tabs.

I tilted my head. "Weeeell, I don't know." She dropped her hands as I approached her. "I'm really good with my hands. Let me provide my expertise." I crowded her personal space. She smelled fantastic. Feminine. I'd had the stank of prison up my nose so long I thought my olfactory senses were permanently damaged—not to mention the smell of the water from the drainage ditch that had attached itself to my nose hairs.

I leaned my head in closer to hers. She licked her lips. And when the tip of her pink tongue darted out, I got hard. Such a small, innocent thing on her part, but after being with Jordy two nights ago, I wanted her more than ever. I unfastened the vest with some quick rips of Velcro then lifted it up over her head.

She still had so many clothes on, screaming seemed appropriate. I refrained, though. Instead, I closed my eyes and groaned. I'd thought the last time we were alone together would've been our last, but this was definitely it. Shouldn't a meaningful conversation be on my mind instead of sex? Shouldn't I be telling her everything I'd kept bottled up for three and a half years? Yes. For sure.

Despite the sexual beast in me, I wondered if a quick fuck was out of the question. I wouldn't, nor could I, ask her for anything when I'd endangered her life just by being alive.

"What's wrong?" she asked.

"Nothing. I'm fine."

She caressed my cheek with her hand. "No, you're not. Where did you stay last night?"

"A bar."

She nodded. "I can't say I blame you for wanting to get drunk."

"I wasn't drunk, but I might be working on a double concussion." Confusion washed over her face, creasing her brow. "You know that long story I was telling you about?"

"Tell me."

"Some dude—you remember Barrett?"

"Jacob Barrett? The wife beater? What happened?"

I smiled. "He decided it was the right time to kick my ass. Except in this case, his buddy hit me upside the head with a bottle."

She giggled. And honestly, it was so ludicrous, it *was* funny. "Oh, my god. What the hell?"

"I know, right. His ol' man is cool, though."

"So, you ended up at Chet Barrett's dive?"

I nodded. "You know the place?"

"I'm familiar but it's not somewhere I hangout or anything."

I scratched my head. "What have you been doing these last three years?"

She smiled and her eyes seemed to sparkle. "Like I said, not much socially."

"I'm sorry you haven't had much of a life since…" *We broke up.*

"Since your unfortunate incarceration."

I chuckled. "Extremely unfortunate. But I was going to say, since we broke up."

"I don't know if we actually broke up. We'd be married already if things had worked out the way they were supposed to."

I groaned and clutched my chest. "Add salt to my wounds, please. I love how it hurts."

She tapped my chest. "Whatever, you know it's true."

I grasped her hand and brought her palm to my lips. Her eyes met mine and I was right back where I was minutes earlier. Imagining myself in her pants. I pulled her closer to me, so our bodies were touching. My hands encircled her waist. She held onto my upper arms. I leaned in for a kiss but didn't close the last few inches, focusing my gaze on her mouth.

Jordy wet her lips. "Aren't you going to kiss me?"

"Uh-huh. I wanna do more than that." I slid my hand down my abdomen and cupped myself. "I want to fuck you." I squeezed my eyes shut. "And I know, I don't deserve—"

"Enough."

"—you. I'm sorr—"

"Kane. Shhh. Enough. I want you, too. As devastated as I was, I get it now, as I got it two nights ago. You were protecting me, which makes you a hero. So please, stop villainizing yourself." Placing her hands on my chest, she rose to her tiptoes and kissed me gently on the mouth.

* * *

Jordana

Kane seemed genuinely surprised that I still wanted him. He touched his lips with his fingertips. His pupils flared and he kissed me again. He picked me up and I wrapped my legs around his hips. Then he carried me to the bed. Even though I was still wearing my boots and most of my uniform, he laid me out before him, admiring my body as though I were naked. His eyes raked over my covered breasts and hips.

"Um, you realize I still have all my clothes on, right?"

He chuckled. "May I?" he asked, holding the hem of the white T-shirt I wore under my uniform.

"You may. And thank you for asking."

He peeled my shirt off slowly. I helped by stretching my arms above my head. Through my sensible cotton bra, he circled one of my nipples with his middle finger. I gasped. My hips undulated with the ripples of tingling pleasure. My eyes stayed fixed on his face, driving up the intensity of my arousal.

He yanked his shirt off. I ran my palm down his front, over his hard muscled chest and abs. Farther down still until my hand met the waistband of his jeans. I undid the button and slid my hand inside, finding his smooth hard cock.

Kane moaned while I stroked him. He rolled to his back and unzipped his fly. Moments later he grasped my hand. "Keep doing that and I'm going to come, and I want to be in you when I do."

I sat up and kicked off my boots. They each landed on the floor with a thump. My pants were next to go, followed by my bra. Kane got rid of his clothes in seconds. He hovered over me, between my thighs, licking and sucking my nipples. "Do you think this place has any condoms?" he asked.

"I dunno. Look in the nightstand."

Reaching over next to the bed, he pulled the drawer open. "Thank god," he whispered. He tore a foil wrapped condom off a long strip of them and rolled it on. "Now, where were we?"

"I think you were about to get me completely naked."

He sat back and drew my panties down. I loved when he took them off for me. There was something so sexy about the way his face lit up with the final reveal. His thumb found my—

I parted my lips and let out a gasp. My body trembled as he pleasured me. I was close to orgasm when he suddenly stopped.

"Why did you stop? I thought you wanted—" *Me*.

"Is this a scar?" he asked with his hand on my lower belly.

I froze, unprepared to tell him about our daughter. "I, uh, had to have some surgery." This wasn't a lie but not the whole truth. My uterus ruptured when I gave birth to Ava. There had been no other way to stop the bleeding except for a hysterectomy.

"Are you okay?"

"I'm fine."

"What kind of surgery?"

"Hysterectomy, but I'm okay with it." He looked at me like he didn't believe me. "Really, it's fine." I pulled him closer and lifted my head to kiss him. He kissed me back, but I sensed his mind was somewhere else. "Stop thinking about it and come inside me.

"Jordy." He said my name with pain in his voice.

"Please, I need you here with me." I thrust my hips until I felt his cock against my core. He sucked in a breath. "Come back to me, Kane."

He weaved his fingers into my hair. "I'm sorry you had to face that alone."

I nodded. "It's okay, I'm tough."

"Yes, you are." He brushed his lips over mine then slid his cock deep inside me. For as many months we had spent apart, all the time and distance nearly disappeared again. The secret I kept from him prevented me from fully enjoying the moment. I was the worst. A total hypocrite. I preached about honesty and telling the truth but continued lying to Kane.

Even though this reunion was temporary, I feared losing him again. Our love story was a tragedy.

Chapter Twelve

Kane

I couldn't get enough of Jordy. I gazed down at her and smiled. Being with her again, even if for one last time, was more than I could've hoped for. This marked the second time we'd been in bed together since my escape. I didn't dare dream of a repeat and jinx myself.

"You're all smiles. Whatcha thinking about?" she asked.

I thrust my hips. "I'm just happy."

She moaned softly. "Me, too. If only this night could last forever."

Me, too. "Let's make this count, then."

I rolled us over, putting her on top. She placed her hands on my chest and swirled her hips.

I came. I passed out. Okay, I didn't lose consciousness, but I couldn't remember my name anymore, which didn't matter because I forgot the alphabet.

The morning came too early, the sun peeking through the gaps in the curtains. I squinted up at Jordy, who stood beside the bed dressed in her uniform. But what else would she be wearing? Neither of us had a change of clothes.

She leaned over and kissed me on the lips. "I'm going to stop by the house and grab something else to wear for both of us on my way to work."

"I don't think that's a good idea."

"I'll call and see if someone from the department can meet me there."

I scrubbed my face with my hand. "I don't like it."

She waved dismissively. "I'll be fine."

I took a deep breath. "Fine. Do what you gotta do."

"What are your plans for today?"

"Hang out here. Twiddle my thumbs." *Pray you don't find me dead.* "Wait for Ryan, I guess."

"Are you going to turn yourself in if he shows up?"

"Not yet. But I do think it would be best for everyone if I did." Jordy told me that Ryan was going to get in touch with the FBI about the possibility of making a deal with the federal prosecutor for more information regarding the bank heist. I was hoping to get a reduced sentence; however, I wasn't holding my breath. Either way, it was time to tell my story. The way I saw it, this might be the only thing that could protect Jordy and Eric.

She grimaced. "I'd rather you not tell me what's best for me."

"Yes, ma'am. When do you think you'll be back?"

"Not sure. I'm going to visit Eric again after work.

See if he's awake enough to talk so I can yell at him." She headed for the door, muttering about wanting to scream at her father for being an asshole.

I chuckled to myself as the door shut behind her. The man was an ass.

I slept another hour after Jordy left. I showered even though I had to put the same clothes back on. Since I was unable to verbalize everything I wanted to say to Jordy, I sat down at the kitchenette table with a small pad of paper and a pen I found in a junk drawer.

Dear Jordana,

I have so much to tell you. So much love for you—

"God, you're so fucking cheesy." I ripped the sheet off the pad, crumpled it, and tossed it in the trash. On a fresh sheet, I started again and wrote three pages. I tore them out and folded the pages in half.

At one fifteen in the afternoon, my stomach growled loudly, demanding to be fed. I had managed to get some one-dollar bills from the convenience store before I stole the hat and sunglasses. Falcon Airport must have some vending machines around stocked with junk food.

Scanning the area around the apartment entrance, I stepped into the sun. The sky was cloudless. The gentle breeze warmed my skin. A small twin engine plane taxied down the runway. Once the plane was positioned to take off, it sped away and lifted from the ground. I watched until it disappeared from sight.

My stomach snarled. "Okay, we'll find you some

food. Will that make you happy?"

I wandered over to the open hangar with the big Soar Xtreme sign and peered inside. Over against the side wall stood a couple of vending machines. No one seemed to be around. Thank god.

I fed the soda machine a few bucks and punched in a selection. The bottle of Cola banged its way down. I retrieved the drink and hit up the snacks next for two bags of chips and a granola bar. While eating my first bag of chips, I read a sign on a door next to the junk food dispensers. *Soar Xtreme Skydiving School.* Hmm. I'd never considered jumping out of a plane before. But I kind of wondered, as I stared at the words, what it would be like. Would I lose my shit and pass out the second I leapt out? Or would I love it? Hard to say, since there were a lot of things I never thought I'd do before going to prison.

"Can I help you?"

I jolted and choked on a chip. *Cough.* Shit! *Cough. Cough.* Spinning around, I found a beautiful woman with strawberry blonde hair, eyeing me suspiciously. I smiled, not knowing what else to do.

"Are you okay? I'm so sorry I startled you."

Cough. "Hi—I was just—" *Cough.* Okay, now I was coughing to stall for time. How could I explain why I was loitering?

"Are you my one o'clock? You're late. I'm Emily." she said.

"Uh...I...guess so. Yeah. I'm your one o'clock. Sorry I'm late." Because how else was I going to explain my presence that didn't involve her calling the police? And god knew that was not a complication I needed.

"No worries. Come with me." She unlocked the door next to the vending machines. I followed her inside. "Will this be your first jump?" she said over her shoulder as she led me to a room with some chairs parked in front of a white board.

"Uh, yes."

"That explains the jumpiness." She erased the marker from the board then wrote, *Tandem Jump Basics*.

I guessed I was going skydiving today.

What did you do today?

Oh, I jumped from an airplane and hurled toward the earth at 120 miles per hour.

Is that all? I chuckled at myself.

She spun around, smiling. "Care to share what's amusing you?"

"I was just having a conversation with myself."

"Fair enough. But if I could have about forty-five minutes of your undivided attention, we can get to the fun stuff."

If you considered plummeting to your untimely death fun.

I chuckled again. She looked at me sideways over her shoulder and smiled. I held my hands up in surrender. "Sorry, it won't happen again."

"If it does, you'll have to tell me what's so funny. I love a good laugh."

I liked this woman.

* * *

Jordana

My dad was being released today and I debated if I wanted to see him or not. The anger I felt toward him simmered below the surface. How could he have destroyed my life? Why did I keep asking myself the same question when I already knew the answer? All he had to do was tell the truth. Hell, not tell me anything about the heist. I'd rather not have known. The doubt it placed in me with regard to Kane sickened me.

Of course, if he had been caught, it would have been better to know so maybe then he could have stayed out of prison. And if I was really wishing for stuff, he wouldn't have done the crime in the first place.

As I drove farther away from the airport, I let the car take me where it wanted to go. I wasn't conscious of driving to the hospital until I pulled into the parking lot.

On the elevator I pushed the button for the correct floor. What was I going to say to my dad? I didn't hate him. I only wished things were different. That he was different.

My mom warned me to protect myself from him, but I never listened.

My father's distinctive voice carried down the hallway to where I had gotten off the elevators. I cringed. Clearly, he was upset about something. Crabbing at someone, likely an undeserving nurse. I never realized until this moment how negative he sounded all the time.

I rounded the doorway of his room, waving at the cop leaning up against the wall opposite the open door.

Inside, my dad was standing in the middle of the room, naked. A nurse told him to get dressed. I wondered why the cop wasn't trying to assist her.

She glanced at me, as if for help.

"Why are you naked?" I asked my dad.

"I am dressed."

I shook my head. "Why? Why do you think you're dressed? I can see your—god, really—get dressed!" It was obvious what he was doing. He wanted to stay there, not because he hated prison but because he enjoyed being pampered.

"I am!"

"This ploy isn't going to work. You're not crazy."

"I'm disoriented."

"Oh, so you're self-diagnosing. Okay, well, if you were disoriented, I doubt you'd actually know that."

"Ask me who the President is?"

"Do you even know that?"

"I know who the President is!"

"Okay, then who?"

"I don't know, I'm disoriented."

I laughed; I couldn't help it. "If you're not going to get dressed then I guess you'll be wearing a sheet back to prison or you'll get loaded on the bus bare-ass naked. Because you are going back to prison."

He sat on the bed and sagged into himself. "I'm not leaving."

"You have to." He lifted his head like he was going to speak. I put my hand up. "And if you say you're disoriented again, so help me god."

The nurse left the room, presumably to get reinforcements. The cop stuck his head in the doorway. "Back-up's on its way. He's been at this for over thirty minutes."

I nodded. "Thanks."

"I can't go back. They'll kill me," my dad said, sounding defeated.

"Maybe they can put you in solitary until they figure out who's behind your beating."

"He spoke quietly, "I think one of the guards was behind it."

"Why do you think that?"

"I heard something."

"Heard what?" He didn't know about Kane's escape, as far as I knew.

"I know someone is trying to kill me, and probably that man of yours, too."

Crossing the room, I sat in a chair near the bed. "Put a sheet over your lap, please. I cannot talk to you like this."

He did what I asked. Pressing his fingers to his cheek, he tested the bruises and swelling. I felt bad because I didn't care that someone had jumped him. "The warden said an inmate beat you." I sounded naïve, but I wanted to know what he knew.

"The guard could've slipped him a little incentive."

"Does this guard have a name?"

"I don't want to put you in any danger."

Since when? And too late.

"Give me a break. I can take care of myself."

A couple of prison guards marched in the room with the cop on duty.

"Brooklyn! Get dressed, it's time to go. You were discharged an hour ago," one of the guards barked.

When my father didn't immediately jump to

action, they forced him off the bed and threw a prison uniform at him.

"Get dressed now or we'll do it for you." *And you won't like it* was implied through his tone.

Still, my father only stood there, daring them to make good on their threat. They were happy to oblige. As they seized him, he said, "I was a shitty father."

"I know," I said.

"But you loved the baseball games I took you to."

Huh? He never took me to a single game.

"I bought you that bat once. What was it again? A Louisville? No. It started with an R."

Was he trying to tell me something or was he really disoriented? A bat that started with an R...

"I played softball," I blurted.

They laid his front across the bed and hooked his hands behind his back. "I know," he breathed. "Go."

No problem. I'd seen more than enough of my father than I cared to. Bat that started with an R? I only knew of one: Rawlings. And yes, that was the brand bat he bought me and the only time I could remember him contributing to my upbringing.

I left the hospital armed with a name. I called Ryan on my way to get a change of clothes for me and Kane. He wasn't sure the name would help, but he'd look into it and meet me after work at the apartment.

* * *

I pulled one side of the police tape down that was across my front door and keyed the lock. The deadbolt wasn't engaged. Not a surprise. Entering the house, I heard a shuffling sound.

Pausing, I listened. "Hello?" It was possible someone from the department could be there doing another sweep for evidence.

No one answered so I headed to the basement to get Kane a change of clothes.

The light was already on when I opened the door. *That's odd.* It was a motion-sensing light. Someone had been down there recently. I unsnapped my gun holster and groped for my Glock, forgetting that I didn't have it on me.

Shit.

There was a noise behind me. I turned.

Something struck the back of my head. I listed to the side. My head swam and darkness closed in around me.

Chapter Thirteen

Kane

I boarded a small plane in a jumpsuit, helmet, and loaded with gear. Settling into a seat against the wall of the aircraft, I stretched my legs out. I rubbed the tops of my thighs. *We are really doing this thing.*

"Are you all right?" my skydiving instructor asked.

I swallowed hard. "Uh-huh."

The captain ducked his head in the cockpit. "Don't worry, Emily is the best." He took a seat in the pilot's chair.

As reassuring as that should have sounded, it wasn't now that I was on the rickety plane, and the pilot was preparing this tin can for takeoff. I rested my head against the wall behind me and closed my eyes. If I died, at least it was from a choice I made.

The plane lifted from the runway. The physics of how a plane was able to defy gravity always astounded me. I once heard someone say it was all in the flaps.

We hit a patch of turbulence and the plane shuddered, creaked, and lurched for what seemed like forever. I wondered if it would ever stop. When we reached altitude, Emily stood. "Let's go. Our final destination has arrived." She giggled.

"I can't tell you enough how unfunny that is."

"You signed up for this."

"Yeah. I'm trying to remember why." Like why I didn't tell her I wasn't her one o'clock? Oh right. Prisoner. Escaped. Me.

She shook her head and strapped us together. "You remember what to do, right?"

I nodded and went over my part in all this. We got into position. The air whipped my face, flapping and billowing my jumpsuit through the open door. I'd never been this tense in my life. I death-gripped the bar above the gaping hole in the plane. Okay, the hole was supposed to be there, but still.

My heart pounded. I couldn't make my body move.

"This is our stop. You're a lot bigger than me, so you have to be the one to jump. Like, now!" she shouted over the wind and the roar of the engine.

She was right. Shit or get off the pot. Or, in this case, jump out of a perfectly flyable plane. I wasn't a quitter, though, and we'd already come this far. What a waste of fuel and time for me to chicken out.

Oh, grow a pair, Kane.

I let go of the bar and pushed us off into the open air.

"Holy shiiiiiit!"

I spread out my arms and arched my back to get

my legs into the correct position like she'd explained.

I floated on a cloud. Okay, not an actual cloud, but that was how it felt, suspended by air. Gravity pulling us toward the earth.

My cheeks hurt. Why?

I realized it was because I was smiling. All my problems seemed so far away. And small. They weren't. But this experience was magnificent. Life-altering. Jordy needed to do this.

The deployment of the parachute yanked us upward and my stomach bottomed out. I laughed.

As we floated down, I took in everything I could see. The sky, ground, the hangars, large patches of grass between the runways, where we would land.

I let my mind go blank and my body relax like never before. All the tension in my muscles subsided.

Just before touchdown, I lifted my legs as Emily instructed. Once we landed, the parachute pulled us backward a few feet.

After detaching from my skydiving instructor, I lay on the grass, staring up at the cloudless blue sky.

"So, what did you think?" she asked. "Ready to go again?"

I gave her a thumbs up.

She smiled. "Thought so."

All I could do was smile back.

"Well, take your time and enjoy the afterglow."

I nodded. She walked away and I closed my eyes.

"Bring your gear to the office when you're done basking in the sun," she called from a distance.

"Thank you."

Sometime later, I finally managed to drag my ass off the ground and return the gear. After thanking

Emily profusely, I snuck back inside the apartment around four in the afternoon.

I took a shower and lay in the bed with only a towel around my hips. Even though I hadn't done much that day, exhaustion overtook me, and I fell asleep.

I awoke to Emily standing next to the bed.

"Uh, the fuck! What are you doing here?" I said, as if I had the right to question her.

She crossed her arms over her chest. "I get to ask that, not you. Who are you, really? Because you're not the Jeff who won the charity auction. He just called to reschedule."

How could I lie to the woman who'd given me one of the best non-sexual experiences of my life? "I'm Kane and what I'm doing here is complicated."

"Life's complicated. Tell me anyway."

"To be honest, hiding."

"From what?"

I sighed. "I'd tell you, but I don't want to frighten you. Not that you have anything to fear from me."

She recoiled, backing away.

"Sorry. I know that's exactly what someone with bad intentions would say." I put my hands up in surrender.

Emily took out a cell phone from her pocket. "We just spent all afternoon together in a life-or-death situation so I'm going to give you one more chance to tell me what you're doing here before I call the police."

"Fair enough. But if you're going to call, can you ask for Detective Keith. He knows who I am and can vouch for me. He's the one who said I could stay here." A look of surprise registered on her face. "Do you know him?"

"Yeah. You could say that."

"How well do you—?"

"He's my husband."

"Will miracles never cease? Lyin' Ryan got hitched."

"No one calls him that anymore."

"Good. I didn't think the nickname was deserved."

We both turned toward the sound of footsteps coming up the stairs.

"Emmy?" Ryan said. He gave me the once-over as I was only wearing a towel.

"Nothing's going on," I said.

He waved me off.

"You know this guy?" Emily asked her husband.

"Yes, I do. It's a long story."

"Did you say he could stay here?"

Ryan nodded.

"And?"

"Him and his... um..."

"Fiancée," I said.

"They needed a place to crash for a few days."

"O-kay. Are you going to tell me why?" Emily asked.

"I'd rather not." She glared at him. "You're not going to be satisfied with it being police business, are you?"

"What do you think?"

I chuckled. "Allow me to explain."

"Please don't," Ryan said. "You'll only make it worse."

"I don't care who tells me. One of you start talking," she said.

"I escaped from prison. Someone is trying to kill me and now Jordana. Probably. I need to find out who before I die or go back to prison, where I'll likely be shanked anyway, so I can at least save Jordana."

"You escaped from prison?" Emily said incredulously. "We are harboring a fugitive and you didn't think to tell me?" She glared at Ryan.

He gave his wife a sheepish grin. "I was kinda hoping I wouldn't have to involve you. His life is in danger. And besides, I owed him one."

"For what?"

"He saved my life last night."

Emily's jaw dropped. "Oh my god." She rushed toward him, hugging him tightly. "I didn't know you were in danger last night. Why didn't you tell me?" She smacked him on the shoulder. "How dare you not tell me, Keith?"

"I'm sorry. If I told you, then I'd have to explain, and I didn't want to lie to you. I love you."

"I love you, too. What happened?"

"I went over to Officer Brook—Jordana's house because I wanted to make sure she was all right. Talk to her again without the eyes and ears down at the department. When I got there, someone started shooting up the house and Kane yanked me inside."

"That's scary. Is Jordana okay? What about Ava? If anyone hurt that little girl—oh my god—I can't even fathom losing a child."

The room went silent like the aftermath of a bomb exploding, and everyone near the blast site lost their hearing for a bit. My ears rang.

I looked at a stone-faced and tight-lipped Ryan.

"Who's Ava?" I asked, breaking the deafening quiet. Emily stared at her husband. I stared at her. "Who is Ava?" My stomach tightened. "What child?" Ryan sighed heavily. "Did Jordy have a kid with someone else while I was locked up?"

"No."

"Then who's Av—" I shut my mouth when my brain fully caught up.

"She was five months pregnant when your sentencing went down."

"How old is my daughter?" I asked absently. I could do the math. Roughly three years old. Five months meant she was conceived the night before the heist. Had Jordy been so angry with me, she kept the pregnancy a secret?

I saw her the day before my sentencing. She had been wearing an oversized hoodie, unusual for her. I should have suspected then she was hiding her belly from me. But why?

I sat on the edge of the bed and scrubbed my face with my palms.

Ryan and Emily stayed quiet, allowing the news to sink in.

I missed everything. All of it. The birth, the first word, first crawl, first time she took a step... "Now the box of toys makes sense."

"Box of toys?"

"Yeah, in the basement." The locked room across from the master bedroom was...my daughter's. Ava. My mother's middle name.

"I don't think Jordy was trying to punish you. I honestly believe she was trying to protect you," Ryan said.

I nodded. "Do my parents know?"

"I don't think so."

"Of course not, if she didn't even tell me. But she told you?" I asked Emily.

"The only thing she ever said to me was that Ava's father wasn't in the picture."

"Well, I'm not, so that makes sense."

"She's lovely. Ava. The sweetest little girl."

I was a father. This was…wow. I didn't know enough words to describe how I was feeling. Happy. But that didn't cut it in the slightest. Ecstatic. Amazed. Overwhelmed. All lame words that lacked the proper amount of emotion for finding out I was a father. I'd dreamed of starting a family with Jordy since our first date. But fuck, I'd missed so much of Ava's life. I had to get out of this prison sentence somehow. "You wouldn't happen to have any pictures of her, would you?"

"I do, from the department's annual family picnic. But I'm sorry, they're at home."

"That's okay, I—"

Ryan cleared his throat, lowering his phone. "Agent Watson wants to meet."

"When?"

"Now."

* * *

Jordana

I struggled against the zip-ties that held my wrists together behind my back. Tape covered my mouth, so screaming for help would be pointless. At least now I knew who'd tried to kill Kane. They left me tethered to a chair behind a desk in an office somewhere. Unfortunately, I didn't have a clue where.

The back of my head throbbed. I leaned to the side as a wave of nausea washed over and through me and sloshed around in my stomach. Whatever they'd hit me with was hard enough to cause a concussion. The wave passed. Thank god because it was difficult to keep fully aware of my surroundings with the threat of puking hovering over me.

The office door opened and a mid-fiftyish, auburn-haired man in a suit entered. He sat down on the other side of the desk across from me. His fair skin was peppered with freckles. He took my gun out from under his jacket and checked the clip. My heart sank. Was he planning on killing me? I wasn't unaware of the risks of being a police officer; I'd signed up for it. However, faced with certain death forced me to realize that Ava had not.

Breathing deeply, I tried calming myself, yet all the fear crept in—all the unknowns and possibilities. Would Ava grow up without either of her parents? If I made it out of here alive, the first thing I was going to do was tell Kane about her. Apologize for keeping her a secret, and hope he understood why I had. I steeled myself and focused on the man in front of me. I took mental note of his facial features, the way he talked with a slight east coast accent, and his approximate height and weight. If I survived the day, I wanted to remember him.

"Officer Jordana Brooklyn."

Yay, he knows my name. I glowered at him.

"It seems we have a problem—"

"Mmm! Mmmmm." The tape tugged at my lips while I tried speaking. We didn't have a problem. *You have a problem.*

"What was that?" He stood and ripped the tape from my mouth and sat down.

I winced. My eyes watered. "You're the one with the problem." The charges were adding up. Kidnapping. Assaulting a police officer…

"From my perspective, you're the one with a bigger problem." *Murder. Battery.*

"Do you know how many felonies you've committed today alone? You aren't going to get away with this."

"And what do you think *this* is?"

"You and your crew covering up your role in the robbery." *Killing me.* "You won't find Kane."

He grinned. "I may not know where Kane is yet, but I know exactly where your father is."

"Good for you. So, it was you who paid Rawlings."

His eye twitched. "Your father doesn't know when to keep his mouth shut, even if it's for his own good, does he?"

"If you're trying to threaten him, you're wasting your time. He and I aren't close." Although, that didn't mean I wanted him dead. "He didn't tell me shit. I just happen to know Rawlings is under investigation. But thank you for confirming his involvement." I prayed he bought my bluff.

"Your father is only alive because I wish it."

"Not what I heard. The hit was interrupted by

some other guards who aren't working for you."

"It's only a matter of time before we find Kane. We know you know where he is, and you're going to tell us."

"Good luck."

"It would be a shame if Ava has to suffer for your mistake. And your father's."

My hands balled into fists. The room became a thousand degrees hotter, and rage erupted out of me. "You fucking monster! You better pray I don't get out of here because you'll only wish you were dead when I get through with you! How dare you threaten my child? You sick motherfucker."

"How 'bout you tell me where Kane is, and we'll leave your daughter out of it."

"I don't know where he is!"

"Do I look stupid to you?"

Yes "Was that rhetorical?"

His hand flew across the desk and slapped me. My head knocked to the side and my vision fuzzed. My cheek stung and I moaned.

"I bet Kane would very much like to know he has a daughter you kept hidden from him."

"What's stopping you from telling him? Oh, right, you have to find him first."

He chuckled without humor. "You tell me where Kane is, or I start killing your family members. But I'll tell you what, I'll let you think about it. I have some business to take care of first. One of my associates will look after you while I'm gone."

I hope you have an accident and your dick falls off.

Chapter Fourteen

Jordana

When the ginger in the suit left, I heard whoever was keeping watch over me playing a game on their phone. Now, what felt like hours later, everything had gone silent, save for the din of cars passing on a highway.

"Hello?" I called. "Is there anyone there?"

I heard clothes rustling and a soft thud, followed by a man's voice saying, "Fuck."

"I need to use the restroom." I wasn't lying but was also hoping I'd be able to find a way out.

"Can't you hold it?"

For how long? "No… Please, I have to pee."

"I'm not supposed to let you out of that room."

"I won't tell anyone. Let me have some dignity before your boss comes back and kills me."

He fiddled with the lock and the door opened. A

nerdy guy with stringy, shoulder-length hair and a shaggy beard walked in. He was neither overweight nor skinny, but looked like he spent a good portion of his days behind a computer.

"Thank—"

The man opened a folding hunting knife with about a four-inch blade. "Since I'm doing you a favor, do me one and don't try anything stupid."

Was this because he couldn't handle it if I did? *I make no promises.* "Sure."

He cut the zip ties off my wrists. My arms hung from my shoulders like wet noodles. I shook them out to get some feeling back. They prickled and tingled. Using the desk for support, I made my way to the door. The man's hand came up to the nape of my neck and he pushed me forward into the hallway. I stumbled and fell to my knees. *Ow.*

Now I knew where I was. Westville's abandoned high school. A new one had been built five years ago. However, I had attended this one. A chain link fence had been installed to keep people off the site. Like that was going to work.

"You wanna take a piss or not?"

I got up and followed him to the restroom.

"Hurry up," he said as I slipped inside.

"Jesus." The bathroom had been torn apart. None of the stalls had doors. The first toilet was clogged—with what, I didn't know. I looked up. Ceiling tiles were gone and had most likely ended up in the toilets. Moving on, I found one that seemed to be in decent shape. Did it flush? Who cared? I really did have to go and made quick work of it. I didn't bother flushing.

I scanned the room, searching for anything that could be used as a weapon. The sinks were missing, leaving behind pipes sticking out from the cinderblock wall. Papers and several upturned books were scattered on the floor. In the corner, among cement dust and debris lay a loose metal pipe about a foot long. I'd almost missed it.

BANG!

BANG!

"Whaddya doing in there?" My captor barked through the door.

Raising the pipe like a bat, I stood to the side of the door, against the wall.

The door opened and I swung the steel pipe at his head. He blocked the hit with his arm. I came at him again with a backhanded swing. He blocked the shot again. This time, he grabbed the pipe and yanked it out of my grip. I was thrown off balance. He easily pushed me to the floor. The man chucked the steel tube to the tile with a *klank*.

My teeth gritted from the force of the fall. He kicked me in the ribs. I lost all the air in my lungs. Temporarily paralyzed, I was unable to do anything except gasp. Tears filled my eyes. I lay on the hard floor, desperately drawing in the oxygen I needed.

Straddling me, he reached down, gripped my hair, and punched me in the face. Blood gushed from my nose, running into my mouth. Leaning to my side, I spat. Coughed. Gasped.

Yanking my head up, he placed his knife to my throat. "I said, don't try anything stupid." He pressed the blade against my neck. I didn't think he broke the skin, but I couldn't swallow without the risk. He withdrew the knife and cuffed the back of my head, using me to push himself up.

He stepped over me and I gripped his pant leg, toppling him to the floor. He grunted.

The knife spun across the dusty tile.

We both lunged for it. I reached it first and gripped the hilt firmly. He jumped on my back and wrapped his arm around my neck. I reached around and stabbed blindly, catching him in the shoulder.

"Bitch."

Something sharp pinched my side and I hissed.

I jabbed him again with the knife—the blade pushing into his throat. His grip around my neck loosened so I stabbed him once more. He made a choking sound and rolled off me. I twisted onto my back and kicked him in the hip. He clutched his throat. He was losing a lot of blood, which seeped through his fingers, pooling beneath him at an alarming rate. Reality must have set in because his eyes went saucer-round. A gurgle bubbled out of his mouth.

"Fuck," I whispered. Fatally wounding him had not been my intention. Although, I'm not sure what I expected to happen. Vomit made a bid up my throat for escape. I gagged and covered my mouth. "Sorry. I'm so sorry." Why was I apologizing to someone who would have killed me if I hadn't taken him out first? Women were always apologizing for shit that wasn't their fault. I blamed him for trying to choke me, didn't I?

I lurched for the door, grabbed the handle with both hands, and burst out into the hallway. I keeled over at the waist, catching my breath.

Get it together.

I ran to the closest exit. The double doors were chained shut. I ran back the other way to the exit that was farther away. Also chained. How the hell was I supposed to get out of here? The last thing I wanted or needed to do was go tearing around the entire school looking for a way out.

Maybe I could break a window in one of the classrooms. They were near the ground. I went from door to door. Every room in the hall was locked.

Chains clanked and my already pounding heart raced faster. I swallowed. My breaths became shallow and quick.

Changing course, I headed to the locker rooms and pool area.

The locker rooms didn't have doors, only a winding corridor to get inside, which never felt safe to me as a teenager. Like how much could a door cost?

I sprinted inside the girl's locker room and made it to the pool entrance.

On the other side of the vast tiled expanse, across the dry pool full of desks and chairs—as if the kids had all thrown furniture in there on the last day of school—were a set of double doors leading outside. A chain lay on the floor in front of it.

I sped across the deck and slammed one of the bars down. Miraculously, the door opened.

Sweet freedom. Was being trapped inside the school like how it felt to be in prison? It must have been, because when the door gave way, relief like I'd never known before washed over me.

The high school was situated at the far end of

town, four miles from Falcon Airport. Good thing I was a runner. However, about two miles in, my legs gave out. My knees buckled and I fell sideways onto the front lawn of a large home. One I'd driven past a million times and wondered who lived there. What kind of job did they have to afford such a lavish estate? I could barely afford the house I owned without Kane's salary.

I lay on the grass, unable to get up. My eyes watered. How long would I have to wait until someone noticed me?

A small plane soared overhead. A car drove past but didn't even slow down.

Footsteps whispered over the grass. Rolling to my side, I found a woman walking toward me with a cell phone in hand. "Are you–oh my god, you're a police officer," she said.

"C-call nine-one-one, please."

"I am right now." She dialed and put the phone up to her ear.

I let myself roll onto my back. The sun beat on my face, so I closed my eyes. My head spun, or maybe the earth was spinning out of control. Nausea settled in my stomach. I turned on my side and vomited. Why was I getting sick? Had my body finally realized the trauma it'd been through and was catching up?

I breathed out of my mouth. Sirens wailed in the distance. No. Wait. An ambulance pulled up to the curb. I barely heard the sound of its diesel engine idling. The fumes clogged my lungs. I coughed. *What's wrong with me?*

An EMT was kneeling beside me.

Talking. His lips moved.

What are you saying?

His brow creased. He mouthed what I thought was "What is your name?"

"Jordana."

The man shook his head and talked over me. His words didn't make any sense, but at least I heard him this time. "Officer Brooklyn?"

Someone shook my shoulder.

"Jordana. Stay with me…"

Chapter Fifteen

Kane

Agent Latasha Watson entered the storage facility at Falcon Airport, two hundred yards from the Soar Xtreme hangar. She was tall and wore her hair in braids down to the middle of her back. The first thing I noticed about her was her no-nonsense expression and confident poise. I liked her.

She walked past the rows of shelving units weighted down with plane parts and brown boxes, some splitting at the corners and others looking brand new. There was a plane engine held up by chains hanging from the steel rafters near where Ryan and I stood.

"Good to see you, Detective Ryan," she said with a tight yet warm smile. "Mr. Adler, we meet again. So, let's get right down to it. Why shouldn't I be putting you in handcuffs right now?"

"I'm ready to talk."

"Why now?"

"I'm sick of the bullshit and don't want to live my life on the run."

"Ryan tells me someone is trying to kill you. Who do you think it is?"

"Whoever masterminded the heist. I know the players, but not the coach. I've only seen the big guy. Don't know his name."

"Would you recognize him if you saw him?"

"Yes."

"Figured. Give me the name of the others and I'll see what pans out." She handed me her cell open to a blank note. I typed in the names, hit save, and handed her back the phone. She slipped it into her pocket.

There was a soft click. A sound all too familiar. Morrison, armed with a gun, rounded one of the tall racks filled with plane parts.

"Get down!" I shouted, lunging for Latasha. Morrison and whoever was paying him weren't going to stop hunting me until I was dead. Maybe prison was safer.

More gunshots.

Ryan ducked behind the engine for cover and returned fire.

It was Watson who fired the kill shot, nailing Morrison in the chest. He crumpled to the floor.

"I'll do a sweep," Ryan said.

Latasha dropped her gun and clutched her arm. Blood ran down the back of her hand.

"You're hit."

"It's not bad. Here," she said, giving me her phone. "Call it in and get out of here."

"You sure?"

"Yeah, I only told one person about this meeting."

Fuuuck.

* * *

Morrison had come without backup. Thank god. I hadn't heard from Jordy since that morning, which was understandable to a point, as I didn't have a phone. Except it was past the time I would've expected her to return. What if Morrison had gotten to her first? Although she was a strong, capable person, my instincts told me something wasn't right.

The sun went down and there was still no sign of Jordy. Where was she? I paced for a few minutes then sat on the bed, wringing my hands. God, I couldn't sit around waiting. I grabbed the apartment key and headed for the exit.

Ryan came up the stairs, calling my name. "You here?"

"Yeah."

"Going somewhere?"

"I was going to look for Jordy. She hasn't shown up yet."

He checked his watch. "It's after six. When were you expecting her? I would have thought she'd be here by now."

"She should have been," I said.

"Have you called her?"

"I don't have a phone."

Ryan had his phone up to his ear two seconds later. He lowered it. "Straight to voicemail. Was she stopping anywhere on her way here?"

"She wanted to swing by the house this morning but told me she'd have someone from the department meet her there."

Ryan huffed and made another call. He asked whoever answered if Officer Brooklyn was still there. "I see, all right…no…shit. Can you transfer me to the chief?"

"What's going on?" I demanded, getting to my feet.

"She didn't show up for work today."

Pangs of dread punched me in the gut. "They fucking took her!"

"We don't know that yet."

"I do. The big boss would want an insurance policy for if and when Morrison failed to take me out."

Ryan waved me off. "What?" he said into the phone. He relayed the information he was getting from the chief. "She's been taken to Westville General for a stab wound."

"How bad?" Fear panged my heart. A stab wound, I hadn't expected. What the fuck happened?

"She's in surgery."

I jumped off the bed. "Let's go."

"How the hell you think that's gonna go? You're a fugitive. Your face has been all over the news."

"I don't give a fuck."

"I do. Your ass isn't the only one on the line here. I happen to love my job and freedom. And Jordy's a great cop and the mother of your child."

"You're right. I'm sorry." I held up my palms and sat my ass back down on the bed.

Ryan tossed a flip phone onto the mattress. "I'm

giving you this per Watson's request. She'll be calling you. Soon. Don't call the hospital; I'll call you when I find anything else out." He headed for the stairs. With his back to me, he said, "Latasha is alive because of you. She wanted me to tell you thanks."

"I didn't do anything."

Ryan made an amused sound. "You pushed her out of the way. Thanks to you, she took that round in the arm instead of the middle of her back."

"I didn't mean for anyone to get hurt. It's what I tried to avoid." My voice cracked.

"You should have come to me three and a half years ago. Things could've been different."

"For what it's worth, I'm sorry."

Ryan nodded and trotted down the steps.

* * *

Jordana

I didn't realize the sting in my side had been another knife puncturing me. Miraculously, it missed everything vital, but bled a lot. And running two miles in the heat didn't help the situation one bit.

I lay in a hospital room in darkness, apart from the bathroom nightlight, on pain meds and wide-awake. How could I sleep? Tears rolled across my temples, soaking into the pillow. A sob wracked my body.

The only good thing was my parents taking Ava somewhere safe. I missed her like crazy, but not enough to risk her life.

My tears were for Kane. Ryan stopped by to see how I was doing and said he'd told Kane not to come.

I needed him, though.

A nurse entered the room. "Hi," she said, softly.

"Hi," I croaked back.

She came over and checked on my IV bag. "I heard you crying. Are you in any pain?"

"Yeah."

"Let me speak with the doc—"

"Drugs won't help the kind I'm in. Thanks, though," I said through a lump in my throat.

She smiled crookedly. "I'm sorry. Is there anything I can do?" This was what I loved about nurses: their bedside manner.

"Not unless you have a time machine." This made me think of Kane more. He loved watching *Dr. Who*.

"I have a few minutes. Would you like me to sit with you?"

"I'd like that. What's your name?"

"Elenore."

"That's pretty."

"Thank you." Elenore sat quietly in the chair next to my bed. Her presence calmed me, and her silence was soothing. I concentrated on breathing in and out of my nose. In. Out. In. Ouuut…

I felt a gentle squeeze on my thigh. I opened my eyes, expecting to find the nurse there. Instead, Kane was crouched on the floor beside the bed. His head was near mine, just above the mattress. He had on a baseball hat underneath the hood of a gray sweatshirt with a Soar Xtreme logo. My eyes sprung leaks. Kane didn't cry much; nonetheless, he was visibly distraught. "Are you really here?" I asked.

"Uh-huh. I had to see you. What happened?"

Waving him off, I squeezed my eyes shut and

more tears fell. He took my hand and kissed the back of it. "I wish I wasn't always so good at making you cry."

"You weren't always good at it. You used to make me laugh."

"Seems like a lifetime ago."

"Maybe it was."

"Is it too late for us?" He cast his eyes down.

"I don't know…but I still love—"

"I love you."

"—you."

He surged up and kissed my lips, lingering for a second or two. "I promise I'm going to make this right."

I nodded. "You should leave before you get caught." Yet I didn't want him to leave. I never wanted him to leave.

* * *

Kane

Jordy looked so small and fragile in the hospital bed. "I don't want to leave you alone."

"You're not. This place is full of people."

"Not your people." *Not me.* I searched her face. Who did our daughter resemble the most? Her or me?

I struggled between asking her a million questions about the ordeal she'd been through and keeping my mouth the fuck shut. Ryan would have grilled her anyway already. I'd closed the analytical part of my brain off while in prison. I didn't want to think too much about the place or how I ended up there. Or how I could've played things differently. Made better choices.

The silence stretched between us. We stared at each other.

"Ryan told me not to come."

She nodded.

"Did he tell you what happened at the meeting with Watson?"

"No. He didn't even say you had a meeting."

I tried not to be annoyed with Ryan but ended up rolling my eyes. "He probably didn't want to burden you."

"How'd it go?"

"Someone showed up to take her out, or me. I really don't know who the bastard was aiming at. Probably all three of us."

Her brow crinkled. "Who all knew about the meeting?"

"That's just it. She said she only told one person."

"Who?" we said at the same time.

"I guess her boss," I said, shrugging.

"Well, either he told the wrong person or he's involved."

It scared me to think how far up this went. How safe was Jordy in this hospital? I had easily snuck past the security stationed on this floor. Ryan let it slip they were shorthanded at the department, which explained why a cop wasn't guarding her room—and how I was able to risk sneaking in to see her. "I don't think it's safe for you here."

"I'll be fine. It's you I'm worried about."

"Jordy, I want Ava to see her mother again. It's bad enough that her old man is a convict."

She gasped and sat up abruptly. Her face contorted in pain. She hissed. "Ow, ow, ow."

"Easy, sweetheart. It's okay. Lie back. You don't want to pop your stitches."

She eased back down. "How did you know?"

"Ryan."

She tried sitting up again but didn't get far. "I—let me explain."

"I'm not angry, and I don't blame you for keeping her from me. I wouldn't have wanted you to bring her to see me in there like that, anyway."

"You aren't mad?"

"Believe it or not, I really do love you. Am I disappointed you never told me? A little. Hurt? Yeah. But I—"

"I didn't want you to be any more miserable than you already were. I saw the look on your face when I visited the final time."

"You have no idea. That place. You can lose yourself in there."

"Did you…lose yourself?"

"God, I hope not. I saw myself as an outsider there."

"I'm sure you were treated that way, too."

"Jordy, I don't think you should stay here. It's not safe. We don't know who—"

She sighed. "I'm not in any condition to leave." She lifted her arm with the IV taped to her hand.

"Well, then I'm staying, too."

"You can't."

"Not up for debate."

"Neither is you leaving. Go." She pointed toward the door with a finger.

Did she really want me to leave? I stared at her.

"Look, I don't want you to go, but I don't want you to get arrested, either."

"I'm going to wind up back in prison either way. You know that, don't you?"

"That doesn't mean we won't figure out who wants you dead first. Now go before I hide you under these covers."

I moaned. "I can't tell you how much that appeals to me." I stood and kissed her goodbye. Little did she know, I wasn't going far.

Chapter Sixteen

Kane

As luck would have it, I was given one more night with Jordy. She was discharged from the hospital and Ryan brought her to the apartment. We figured the airport was still the safest place to hide out. I did my best to make sure she would be comfortable. She was still a little sore from the stabbing. Emily came by with extra pillows and some carryout for us from Jordy's favorite Italian restaurant.

I went to the bathroom and when I came out, Jordy appeared at the top of the stairs in a pair of leggings and an oversized sweatshirt. Her hair in a messy bun. No makeup. Just the way I liked. I might have lost my man card for admitting this, but my heart fluttered like it was full of those flying insects with colorful wings. Okay, okay, it was full of butterflies.

"Hi. I would've carried you up the stairs."

She smiled. "Totally unnecessary and besides,

they are too narrow, I think."

"You look beautiful." And she did. More than ever.

Although she missed Ava, Jordy wouldn't risk our daughter's life by letting her stay in town. She'd ordered her parents to take her to their vacation home across the state border. She told me she had FaceTimed Ava from Ryan's car on the way over.

I wanted to meet Ava, but not like this. Not over the phone, and not when I was going back to prison so soon. My job as a father was to protect my child, if even from myself.

She blushed. "I'm sorry. Do you mind if I sit down?"

"Come," I said, offering my hand to her. "Emily made up the bed for you." I led Jordy over to the bed. She got in and sat up against the headboard, surrounded by pillows.

"Wow. I don't think I've ever been in bed with this many pillows before. She did an awesome job."

"Are you hungry? She brought food, too."

"Starved."

I made up a tray of the pasta and garlic bread and set it on her lap.

"Aren't you eating?"

"In a minute."

She smiled and picked up her fork. After we finished, I cleared the plates and washed them.

"Such service. I don't think I've ever seen you do dishes."

I smiled at her over my shoulder from the kitchen sink. "What are you talking about? I did the dishes all the time."

"Did you?" She giggled.

"Yes, and I was assigned to food services in prison at first and washed the trays and the cooking pots n' shit."

"That sounds horrible."

I dried my hands with a paper towel. "It was. Now I'm in the education department. Well, at least I was. I'll probably be on dish duty again when I go back."

"Education?"

"Yeah, I was tutoring some guys for the GED."

"That sounds fulfilling to some degree."

"It was. When they passed, and even when they didn't. I was surprised how many people can't read."

"Maybe when you get out, it's a career path to consider."

I shrugged. "Never thought about it." I wasn't qualified to be a cop anymore, which made me a little depressed. Sighing, I came over to the bed and sat down.

"Uh-oh. I know that sound. Talk to me. Whatcha thinking about?"

"It's depressing knowing that I can't be a cop anymore."

"Let's change the subject, then. Come here and sit next to me." I waggled my eyebrows at her and she smiled. "Not for that, I just want to be near you for as long as we have left."

I crawled to the head of the bed and settled in on her uninjured side. She weaved her fingers through mine. "What's Ava like?" I asked. I didn't know anything about my own daughter.

"Beautiful, funny, smart, and stubborn like you."

"What does she like to do?"

"Color. Well, scribble crayon all over the pages of her coloring books and call it coloring." Jordy laughed. I'd forgotten what that sounded like.

"Does she have your laugh?"

"She has a little girl laugh and voice right now, so it's hard to tell. Oh, she's very girly, which is cool. Loves wearing dresses."

"So, she's not a closet dress-wearer like you."

"No. She'll wear pants but, given the choice, it's a dress all the way."

"I hope I get to meet her one day."

"What are you talking about? You will."

"Jordy, you're going to have to face the fact that it might not be until she's ten years old. At least."

"Now I'm depressed."

I turned and faced her. "I need to tell you something, but I have trouble finding the right words, so I wrote you a letter. I'd rather you not read it in front of me, though."

"Why? If it's from the heart, I'll love your words no matter what they say."

"Even if it's something you don't want to hear."

"Now I have to read your letter. Where is it?"

I inched off the bed and retrieved the folded papers that I'd stuck to the fridge with a magnet. I brought them to the bed. She looked up at me and my lopsided smile.

"Can I have the letter, please?" She held out a hand.

I placed the lined yellow pages on her palm, then went and sat on the end of the bed, facing away from her.

The papers rustled then she cleared her throat. Oh,

god, she was going to read it aloud.

"Dear Jordana…"

* * *

Jordana

"The first time I saw you was the first day of police academy. You walked in with your head held high, even though you were one of only two women in that room. I remember your hair was pulled back in a ponytail. I don't think I heard one word the instructor said. I was too busy staring at you from the back. All I could see was your profile, but it was enough. Then you raised your hand to ask a question and I heard you speak for the first time. Your voice and reserved smile were a contradiction to the job we were training for. I tell you this because it was the moment I fell in love with you."

Kane lifted his head from the low hang he'd been rocking. "It's true."

"I believe you."

I continued reading his letter. *"I stopped you after class that night and asked you out, right in the parking lot. You seemed shocked and kept stealing glances at me. You were so shy, which made me want to get to know you more."*

My cheeks were heating up now. "That's because you're gorgeous, and I was nervous, and just looking at you embarrassed me."

"Why would it be embarrassing?"

"Because of how inexperienced I was. I thought you could tell."

Kane snort-chuckled. "I didn't know then. I just thought you were very shy."

I took a deep breath and read on. *"On our first date, you couldn't eat anything at dinner, and that's when I knew you were as nervous as I was."*

"I was more nervous, by the way," I interjected.

"I know. Finish." Kane ran his fingers through his hair.

"I learned so much about you that night. How old you were when your parents divorced. The reason you wanted to go into law enforcement. What a crappy father you had. Later, when you told me you were a virgin, just knowing what he put your through made me realize why. You never found yourself able to trust a man enough to give yourself to one. I promised myself that I would never put you in a position not to trust me. But I failed you. I promised myself to always make you feel loved and appreciated, and never to abandon you. But I failed on all accounts."

Tears welled in my eyes. My chin quivered.

"I'm so sorry, Jordy. There are no words to express how much I love you and don't deserve you. My wish for you, when I'm put away again, is that you find someone who is worthy of your love and treats Ava like a true father should. Like I would, if I had the chance. I love Ava, too, even though we've never met. I can't explain it but there's something about having a child, even if you don't know them. I want to know her but the harsh reality that I must

face is I may never."

A sob left my throat. I wasn't sure I could keep reading. I wanted to yell at him for even thinking he wouldn't get to know his daughter. That we wouldn't be together in the end. That we would never get married. Have a life living under the same roof again.

Except, I had to admit to myself that he could be right. I sucked back my tears. He was still sitting with his back to me, his head hanging off his shoulders even lower than before.

"I can't imagine what you went through these last three years. I'm sorry I wasn't there for you. You are amazing. You are strong. You are brave. You are a survivor. And even without seeing it, I know you are a great mom to our Ava. Please continue to be all the things I know you are after I'm gone.
"I will always love you. Kane."

I moved to the end of the bed and hugged Kane from behind. "After you're gone. What does that mean?"

He put his hands over mine. "You know what it means."

"I'm not even considering it. Nope. We're going to find out who's behind all this before that happens."

"And if we don't?"

"I'll find them and slice them up into—"

He laughed quietly. "You will not. That isn't your way."

"Well, my way sucks."

"Doing the right thing doesn't suck."

"Yes, it really does." I clung to him for a long

time, resting my head on his shoulder. "What if you're right and we never see each other again?"

"Tell Ava that I'm sorry that we never got the chance to be a family." I kissed the side of his neck and he gasped.

"I thought you were sore?"

"I am but I don't care. I want to be with you. We both know we might never get another chance."

He turned around and I moved back up the mattress to make room for him. He came toward me with heavily-lidded eyes. I took my clothes off, starting with my sweatshirt. He peeled his shirt off and shucked his jeans.

"I don't want to hurt you. Let me know what position will be most comfort—"

I put my index finger to his lips. Then I kissed him until we were both panting. I rolled him to his back and straddled his hips. He squeezed my bottom in his hands and rolled my hips forward. Heat flooded between my legs and the friction nearly made me orgasm.

Kane looked up at me and smiled. "Shy woman no more."

"Only with you." He was the only one who had ever made me feel beautiful. The only one I felt I could trust, but then again, I never really had fully trusted anyone, had I? I hated myself for trusting the one man who had always lied to me instead of the one who never had.

Never again would I doubt this man.

I took Kane inside me, and we made love for what I hoped wasn't the last time. No one could predict the future. But it didn't look like sunshine and rainbows on the horizon.

168

Chapter Seventeen

Kane

"Does the name Rawlings mean anything to you?" Ryan asked me on the way to our second meeting with Watson.

"I'm not familiar with the name. Who are they?"

He made a right turn before answering. "Jordy gave me the name. The guard who turned a blind eye to Eric's beating. He hasn't been at work since the attack. I'm thinking he's already—"

"Dead," we said at the same time.

"Who the hell would be able to pay or pressure guards from multiple prisons to do his work?" I said.

"I know, right? Who the fuck is this guy?" Ryan was referring to the big boss man behind the heist. He flipped on his blinker then turned left toward the FBI field office. I wasn't thrilled about meeting Watson there, but if her boss was the Duke, then at least I could ID him. She made sure the man was at work this morning before inviting us.

My knee bounced up and down. Today I was going back to prison after my interview. I couldn't be more excited, said no one. Ever.

Ryan parked in the covered garage and killed the engine. He focused on the concrete wall. "Watson wanted me to text when we got here so she can escort us inside."

"You mean escort me."

He smiled. "Yeah. In case someone recognizes you."

I tilted my head back against the seat and took a deep breath. "I'm not ready to go back to prison."

"Is anyone ready to go in the first place?"

I chuckled. "Fuck no."

"Man, it must suck so bad for you in there."

"Yeah, I'm a walking cliché."

"So, it's true what they say, huh?"

"What? Convicts hate cops? Yeah, you could say that."

"The inmates pick fights with you? How often?"

"Weekly. At first almost daily. There's this big fucker everyone calls Monster who just won't leave me alone. I don't like to brag, but I'm his favorite punching bag."

Ryan laughed. "I'll bet. But you've put on quite a bit of muscle since I saw you three years ago."

"I can hold my own."

He texted back and forth with Watson. "She said to meet her at the doors."

We got out, me taking my time.

I followed him to the door to the main building.

"You were a great cop, you know? And friend. This shit was so hard to swallow. Good cop gone bad.

It never made sense.”

“Now you get it.”

He nodded. “I don’t know if you had another choice, either.”

“Oh, that reminds me.” I fished a folded piece of paper out of my pocket and handed it to Ryan.

“What’s this?”

“Open it.”

He complied and read the name I’d written down. “Rodney Javernick. Who’s…?”

“The son of someone I owe a favor to. Ray Javernick.”

“So, why are you giving it to me?”

“You’re the detective. Look into him. He disappeared without a trace. Cops ruled it a suicide, but Ray doesn’t think so. He might be wrong and that’s fine. He just wants to know the truth.”

Ryan nodded and put the piece of paper in his pocket. “I’ll do what I can. Although sniffing around some other cop’s old case might get their panties in a wad.”

“You can handle the heat.”

He laughed. “You have a point.”

The door opened from the inside. Agent Latasha Watson stood just on the other side of the threshold with her arm in a sling. She made eye contact with me. “Good, you’re wearing your hat and sunglasses. Should make our passage easier.”

Our passage into Hell.

She stepped aside and we followed her down the hallway to the end, then down another corridor. Agents nodded at her along the way. Watson entered a room with a metal table and three chairs. I took note of the drywall since this was probably the last time I'd see any for many years. Lots of cinder block walls were in my future.

"Have a seat," she said, indicating the chairs on the other side of her, farthest from the exit.

I plopped down. "Thank you for not cuffing me."

"It's only a courtesy. Don't make me regret it."

I smiled. "I won't." I thought about saying something snarky, but she was the one holding any chance of getting my sentence reduced.

She'd been carrying a brown folder under her sling. Presently, she laid it on the table and opened it. "The names you gave me checked out. Turns out, one of them was on the FBI watchlist for firearms. A team raided his house this morning. Arrested him and the other four on your list."

"Tell me they seized evidence, too, and won't be kicked free."

"You bet your ass. A lot of it, but none of them would give up their boss. At least not yet."

"Did they deny he exists?"

"No, one of them coughed up that he was concerned for his safety, especially in prison."

"Interesting," Ryan said.

"Yeah, it is," she said. "As for Rawlings, he's a piece of shit. Don't even know how he got hired. We are looking for him now."

"I don't think you'll find him," I said. "Not alive, anyway."

"I think you're right."

Maybe Watson's boss wasn't involved. He had to know all this by now, didn't he? "So, you don't think your boss is involved?"

She adjusted her position in the rigid chair. "No, I don't. But I would still like to rule it out to be sure."

"Does he know I'm here?"

"Not yet."

Obviously, she had doubts if she didn't tell him I was coming in.

"I'd like to record our interview, Mr. Adler."

"Please do."

* * *

I answered every one of her questions, telling her everything I knew, including a description of the heist master, as I liked to call him, or the Duke. Late fifties, if I had to guess. Auburn hair, freckled. God complex. I noticed her eyes flare slightly, yet she said she didn't know anyone matching the description.

Watson stood, gathering the file. "Thank you. I wish you would have told me all this before."

"I'm sorry." Wasn't I apologizing a lot lately?

She nodded. "The prosecutor will probably need you to testify. Even if we don't find the boss, these guys are responsible for several bank heists along the coast. I'll be back in a bit."

After she left, I leaned back in my uncomfortable chair.

"You did good," Ryan said. "I get why you wouldn't say anything during your trial. Sometimes we have to put others before ourselves."

"I needed to protect Jordy…and Ava." Not that I knew about her at the time.

"I did a thing. Kept me from making detective for a minute."

"What'd you do?"

"Went on a ten-sixteen call. Little girl in an abusive situation, nobody wanted to do shit about."

"So, you took a stand when no one else would?"

"Somebody had to protect her from her abusive fuck of a father."

"Good for you. Takes character. You've always had a lot of that."

"You, too."

We sat quietly until the door swung wide and a man entered the room. I didn't recognize him. He had flaming red hair. No wonder Watson seemed surprised by my description of the Duke, except her boss was at least ten or more years younger. Watson rushed in behind him.

He charged at me with a scowl. "Why are these man's hands not hooked behind his back?" he barked over his shoulder at her.

"He's not resisting, and he came in of his own volition."

"He's a dangerous fugitive!"

I am?

A combination of *that's-bullshit* and *give-me-a-break* showed on her face. "He's not dangerous."

"Get up and lock your hands behind your head, Adler."

I grinned in disbelief. All I had been doing was sitting there quietly. Nonetheless I did what he said. The chair screeched over the floor as I stood. I linked my fingers behind my head.

"He saved my life, Bob."

"I'll deal with you later, Watson." Bob tossed the chair out of his way and yanked my arms down one at a time, cuffing my wrists behind my back. "We need transport for the prisoner."

"It's already arranged and waiting downstairs," she said. "Kane, what do you think?" she hinted.

I shook my head no. What an anticlimactic disappointment. Her boss wasn't the Duke.

"Sure?"

"Positive."

"What the fuck are you two talking about?"

No one answered. He pushed me toward the door and out into the hallway.

"I'm meeting with the federal prosecutor," she said. "I'll let you know how it goes."

"Thanks," I said.

Chapter Eighteen

Kane

Fuuuuck. The potpourri of prison filled my nose. The stale air reeked of BO, disinfectant, and dirty sweat socks, mixed with a hint of urine. Ah, home sweet vomit. The door to my new cell slammed shut. The usual metal on metal screech was absent. *Huh?* Maintenance was actually on top of things for once? As if that ever happened. Although, this was odd, I had more significant matters to think about, like why wasn't I put in solitary or moved to the other prison upstate?

The lights were dimmed. I heard rustling on the top bunk and squinted into the darkness. I couldn't see my cellmate's face.

"Hey, I'll take the bottom bunk."

"Piss off."

I knew that voice.

Monster.

"Fuck me."

I always figured that he didn't like me because I was a cop and he saw me as a challenge or maybe even a threat. It was hard to determine if he worked for the Duke. Either way, I dreaded when the big freak woke up in the morning and realized we were cellies.

I plopped my ass down on the bottom bunk, exhausted after my long day and mandatory strip search, which was so much fun. As if I'd hide something under my ball sack. The bunk creaked and shook while Monster tossed and turned.

Jesus, maybe the bed would break and crush me to death. I wasn't sure if that would be better or worse than a shanking.

Closing my eyes, I tried sleeping but spent hours hovering in a semi-conscious state, neither fully awake nor sleeping. I pictured Jordy and Ava waiting for me outside the prison gates when I was released from this hellhole. Would they even be waiting? How much longer did I have to be here? How much longer before someone murdered me in here? Saying I felt a sense of dread was an understatement. Ominous foreboding was more like it. Something bad was going to happen.

And I was whining like a little bitch.

Slowly, I became aware of the cell door opening. The metal clanking roused me, and my eyes cracked open. A figure slipped into the small concrete palace. I didn't bother asking who the fuck let themselves inside. If I hadn't been somewhat awake, I wouldn't have heard them.

It didn't matter. I knew who it was.

Of course this late-night visit was the reason for

the hinges having been greased. So, this was where it happened, where I died. Monster was no doubt in on it, too, ready to hold me down while this figure stabbed my heart and lungs twenty-five times. I prayed Ava would grow up like her mother: strong and with good moral character. Maybe it was better she never got to know me. At least she wouldn't miss someone she'd never met. My only regret would be not getting to see her even once. To hear her laugh, to play tea parties with her, do all the things a father was privileged enough to do. Hug her when she was sad, see her graduate, walk her down the aisle. Hold my grandchildren.

Oh, my god, the life I would never get to lead flashed before me.

I wasn't ready to die.

* * *

Jordana

Ava ran out the front door of my parents' vacation home with her pigtails flowing behind her. I teared up. Crouching to her level, I hugged her like I hadn't seen her in a year. Her hair smelled like strawberry shampoo, the best scent in the world. She clung to me, her little arms clutching me around the neck. I took a shuddering breath. I'd been through so many emotions in such a short period of time, I was a bowl of mush. Picking her up, despite the tenderness in my side, I carried her back into the house.

I sat on the couch with her still in my arms. My mom came over and sat next to us. She rubbed my back and stroked my hair, which only made me cry harder.

"Shh," she said. "Everything is going to be all right." Even though I had a difficult time believing those words, it was exactly what I needed to hear.

Ava let go of my neck. "Why are you crying, Mommy?"

I faked a smile. "Because I missed you so much."

"I missed you, too." She climbed off my lap and ran down the hallway to the TV room.

"So," my mom said, "are you going to tell me what's really going on?"

I took a deep breath and wiped the tears from my face. "Kane."

Her eyes widened and she inhaled.

"I know what you're going to say—"

"Jordana, I don't think you do. I always thought you should have told him about Ava. But that decision was yours to make."

"He's back in prison. I'm worried about him."

"I thought that might be the reason for the tears." She tilted her head to the side. "Understandable, since someone tried to kill him. Will Kane get time added to his sentence?"

I shrugged. "I don't know. He finally told the FBI all he knew about the operation and the people behind the heist."

"Good."

"He was protecting me. They made him work for them."

She nodded. "I always believed he had a good reason for doing what he did."

"They caught everyone now, except for the main leader. The FBI thought it might be one of their own."

"And it wasn't."

"No, so now Kane's back in prison, and who knows if he'll even survive and now Ava may never know her daddy."

"Or before he even knows about her."

"He knows."

Ava appeared at the entrance of the hallway.

"Hi, sweetie," I said.

She came forward, dragging a throw blanket my mom knitted behind her.

My stepfather entered the house through the kitchen. "Hey, kid," he said to me.

Ava climbed onto the couch. She made a production out of lying down and drawing the blanket over her. The girl loved being cozy.

"Hi...Dad," I said. For some reason, although I never called him "Dad," this seemed like the right moment to start.

He smiled warmly with all the love in his eyes that a father should have for his daughter. My own father never looked at me like that. "How you holding up? I spoke with Chief, and he told me a bit about what's happening."

My stepdad still referred to Ryan Keith's father as "Chief," even though the man was no longer the Chief of Police. How he knew anything wasn't much of a surprise. Chief had three sons who were in the police, fire, and rescue business, so of course they would've heard things and talked to their dad. They were a close-knit family that I envied and admired. "I'm doing okay." I exhaled loudly, unable to breathe right.

"Kane's a survivor. How are you doing physically?"

"Sore, but I'll live." I looked at Ava, who watched our conversation with innocent curiosity. I wondered how much she understood. Did she know about daddies? She would ask sooner or later about Kane. "I need to tell you something, sweetie, that you may not understand right now, but you will."

Her eyes lit up. "What, Mommy?"

"You know I'm your mommy, right?"

"Yeah, I love you, Mommy."

"Aw. I love you." She truly was a dear heart. "Do you know what a daddy is?"

"Uh-huh. Emlee's daddy picks her up from Miss Susie's." She mispronounced Emily.

"Emily's daddy picks her up from daycare?"

"Uh-huh. From Miss Susie's house. He's funny."

God, was I about to ruin Ava's life by telling her about her own daddy? What if he never got out of prison alive? She had a right to know, though. "You have a daddy, too. He's been away but I hope you'll be able to meet him someday."

She smiled and sat up straight. "I have a daddy, too, like Emlee?"

"Uh-hm. You look a lot like him, too."

"He looks like me?"

"You have his blue eyes."

She smiled with pride. "When can I see him?"

"I'm not sure yet." I only prayed she would get to see him. I had to stay positive if I was going to get through this.

"Where's my daddy?"

Naturally, she would ask that.

"Well, he's away right now."

She crossed her arms and pouted. And I couldn't blame her because I wanted to do the same.

184

Chapter Nineteen

Kane

The figure approached the bunk. I pretended to be asleep. He got within striking distance. What little light coming in from the cell block glinted off a large blade of some kind. I also glimpsed a prison uniform on the man. But I couldn't see his face.

I lunged off the bed and tackled him to the floor. We grappled for control of the knife. I ended up on my back, blindly punching at him. My right hook caught him in the temple. He grunted and seemed to have a momentary brain glitch, but quickly recovered. His hand came down with the blade. I blocked the downward thrust with my forearm. The tip of the sharp steel grazed my cheek. It may have been deeper than a graze as a warm flow of blood ran, pooling in my ear.

The knife came back at me. I knocked the blade away. Reaching up, I pushed on his throat.

"Get him…off me, Monster," my attacker

growled, "you dumb…fuck."

This asshole was the dumb one. If you wanted someone like my cellmate's help, insulting the man wasn't the best plan. Of course, they must've planned this out ahead of time. But I had a healthy respect for the giant and we traded insults as equals.

I squeezed harder. He made a choking sound and dropped the knife.

His hands wrapped around my neck. "Brock," I wheezed. "A li'l…help." I used his name, hoping this would give me extra points.

"Don't call me dumb and I'm trying to sleep!" Monster roared.

BOOM!

Monster's feet hit the floor. He bear-hugged my attacker around the waist from behind. With a twisting back heave, he flung the figure toward the concrete wall and his head conked the steel toilet on the way to the floor, silencing his verbal protesting. "Who's dumb now, Warden?"

Warden? Warden Maddox? What the fuck? I sat up and leaned against the lower bunk. "Thanks."

Monster grunted. He opened the cell door all the way. More light from the block spilled in, revealing the identity of my would-be killer.

It wasn't Maddox.

The Duke lay on the floor in a crumpled heap in a prison uniform. "Son of a bitch." I knew the prison, especially one of this size, had more than one warden, and I thought I had met all of them. Apparently not.

Monster went over to the warden and kicked his side. "Who are you, calling me—? You're dumb, muthafucker. Now your ass is going to be in here with us." He looked at me. "You know this fool who was fucking with my sleep? Calling me dumb."

"Not his name."

"Yeah, you do. Larson."

I'd heard that name. *Shit*. Well, I felt stupid. Larson was the Complex Warden who oversaw this prison and a couple others in the region. Watson's boss had to have been the leak. Larson probably called him when I escaped custody, and her boss didn't think twice about calling him with an update.

All the lights came on in the cell block. The inmates hooted, hollered, and banged on their cells. Rising above the noise was the distinct sound of the guards marching their way toward us.

Larson moaned.

Brock cold-cocked him in the nose.

Maddox stood in the doorway, flanked by several guards. He glanced down at his boss sprawled on the floor. Looked at us. "What the fuck is going on here?"

"He was messing with my sleep," Brock said.

"Cuff them and sit their asses down," he barked at the guards. Brock and I didn't resist. We sat. The guards remained in the cell. "What, you think you're done?" he said to them.

The guards looked at each other, puzzled. "But he's the warden," one said.

"So? He's wearing a prison uniform. Doesn't this strike you as odd?"

"Yes, sir."

They rolled Larson onto his stomach and hooked his hands behind his back. He groaned.

"Tell me what happened," Maddox said.

"I was sleeping, and Larson came in and woke me up," Brock said.

Maddox shook his head. "I heard you say he interrupted your beauty sleep. Why is the Complex Warden out cold?"

Brock motioned with his head to the shiv lying next to the toilet. The warden took a handkerchief from his pocket and picked up the homemade blade by the sharp end. "His fingerprints better support whatever story you're about to bullshit me with."

Brock and I nodded.

"Mr. Adler, what's the story as you see it?"

"He attacked me," I said.

"Cut you pretty good too from the looks of it."

"Yes, sir. I believe he's the one who planned the transport ambush."

He nodded and addressed the guards. "Unhook the prisoners and get this piece of shit out of here. Put him in the Hole."

"Sir? He's the warden."

"I'm the warden in charge here and he looks like an inmate to me." He stepped over Larson.

"Do me a favor and call Agent Latasha Watson," I called after him as he exited the cell.

The guards uncuffed us and carried Larson out, leaving Monster and I locked in alone.

Brock climbed onto the top bunk. "This doesn't mean we're friends."

"I'll take not friends over enemies any day. Why did you help me?"

"I don't like people fucking with my sleep."

I snorted. "I owe you."

"You're fucking right you do."

"What put you in here anyway?"

"Why?"

"Want to make sure the person to whom I owe one isn't a murderer or worse."

"*Pfft*. Fuck no. Phishing. But the Feds call it identity theft."

Um. Wow, a non-violent offense. Will wonders never cease. Except why was he in max, then? I'd have Jordy look it up for me. "Must have been some scam."

"It was, until we got caught."

"I know Larson messed with your sleep, but why would you really help me? It looked like you were in on the attack."

"You think that fool wouldn't try to pin your murder on me? Our fights are well-documented. Shit. I'm eligible for parole in a year."

"Still?"

"I gotchu, cop. You got me?"

"Yeah." This was now the third person I owed. Ray, Chet, and now Monster.

Chapter Twenty

Kane

I picked up the phone. Jordy sat opposite me behind the glass partition in the visitation room. She smiled. "Hi."

"Hey, you. I took the deal. Six more months."

"I heard. How ya feeling?"

"Anything is better than seven more years. Grateful."

"I still don't understand why you didn't want me to bring Ava."

"I do really want to meet her so badly, but I don't want her to have any memories of me behind bars."

"I don't think she'd remember it."

"But I would, and I don't want that image in either of our heads."

The deal I took was six more months for the escape and a conditional release, provided I testified in court against Larson and his crew.

Were they kidding? No problem. I leapt at the

deal, which was better than I'd hoped for. Agent Watson really helped make this happen. I think she realized this case would make her career. Although, she said that's not why she did it.

"How are you?" I asked Jordy.

"I'm all right. Ava asks about you almost every day. 'When am I going to see Daddy? When is he coming home?'"

"Tell her soon."

"I do, but she's as stubborn as you."

I chuckled. "Did you bring any pictures?"

"Oh—yes." She dug into her purse and pulled out a small photo album. "I made this for you. They probably won't let you have it, but maybe they can give you one of the pictures." Jordy flipped open the cover and put the first photo up against the glass.

I leaned closer to the partition. "Ultrasound."

"Yeah, well you missed a lot. This was at twenty-two weeks."

I appreciated the grainy, gray-and-white printout and marveled at the outline of Ava's face and hand. "That's amazing. I wish I could have been there."

"I know you do. I'm so sorry."

"What are you apologizing for?"

"I don't know. Getting you arrested."

"Jordy, none of this is your fault. I love you more than anything, and I love Ava."

"Of course you do. She's your flesh and blood."

My chest swelled. She was my daughter. "Show me the next picture."

She still had the album plastered to the glass. "Oh," she said, bringing the book down and turning to the next page. The second set of pictures were of

Ava as a newborn. All the pages following were a photographic age progression up until the present.

"The last picture, I took this morning." Ava was leaning against the couch with her feet on the floor. Her bright blue eyes were focused on what I imagined was the TV, her long dark hair held back in a ponytail.

God, I couldn't wait to meet her. "She's beautiful." My eyes watered, but there was no crying in prison. Not gonna happen. "I can't believe you and I created that. Her."

"We did."

I put my palm against the glass, and she did the same so our hands "touched."

"I love you," she said.

"I miss you like crazy."

"Okay. I'll see you in six months." She turned away.

My heart plummeted. "Wait. Jor—"

She swiveled back toward me and smiled.

"Will you come visit me again?"

She giggled. "Of course, silly. I was joking."

"It doesn't have to be every week. Only as long as—"

"This is going to be a long six months, isn't it?" She sighed.

"The longest. But I'll come home. Just make sure you leave the door open for me."

"Always. I never closed it."

Tears spilled from my eyes. *Fuuuuk. Meeee.*

As selfish as it sounded, I was overjoyed to hear those words. By all means, she had every right to forget about me and move on with her life without me. Except, she didn't.

"What's wrong?" she asked, as if she had something else to apologize for.

"Noth—" my voice caught, "…ing. I never thought—I always believed you were done with me. I'm so happy." I wept silently.

"I never let you go."

"I never let you go."

"Good. Now that we got that out of the way, see you in six months."

I laughed out loud. "God, I love you."

Epilogue

Six Months Later

Jordana

My stomach fluttered and my hands shook. I didn't know if it was from excitement, anticipation, or just plain nerves. My anxiety-o-meter's needle was pointed to high.

I wanted to look perfect for Kane's release day, even though he wouldn't care if I picked him up with no makeup on, hair in a messy bun, wearing sweatpants. In fact, the last time I visited I asked him what he wanted me to wear, and he'd said those exact words.

"Mommy, your hand's wet," Ava said.

Great. Sweaty palms.

I glanced down at her little hand in mine. My engagement ring sparkled in the sunlight. Kane hadn't officially proposed again, and I hadn't held him in my arms in six months, yet I was hopeful he still wanted to get married someday.

Only Ava and I were picking him up today, for which I was grateful. His parents wanted to be here and take him to their house (they were still upset with me for not telling them about their grandchild) for a welcome-home party. However, he'd squashed the idea immediately. He wanted to do whatever Ava and I normally did on a Friday afternoon—after taking a long hot shower, of course. So, a trip to the farmer's market for fresh produce for a fruit salad and a backyard barbeque was the plan.

I started going to a therapist to help me work through my "daddy issues" while Kane was serving out the remainder of his sentence. I owed it to myself to learn how to let go of the past and still have a relationship with my father that I could live with. It was taking some time, but I finally was able to visit Eric for the first time last week without feeling drained afterward.

Things started opening up and some guards came outside. I weaved back and forth in my high heels, trying to see if Kane made it out yet. My heart pounded. Did something happen? Was he not coming?

Then he appeared.

He said goodbye to a couple of the DOCs' finest. He was smiling and having a laugh with them. A series of gates opened, and he walked out, a free man.

"Is that Daddy?" Ava broke away from me and ran toward him. A man she'd never met before, only seen in pictures. She didn't care. My normally timid girl did not care. "Daddy!"

Kane strode forward and dropped to his knees.

She ran into his outstretched arms. He hugged her and rose to his full height. She kept an arm around his neck as he settled her at his hip. "I'm so happy to meet you, Ava."

Clearly not knowing how to respond, she said, "We're going to the farmer's market for fruit."

"Oh, yeah, I love fruit. What's your favorite?"

"Strawberries."

"Yum. I love strawberries." It was true. He loved anything strawberry. Shakes, pie, cheesecake. Anything.

"You do?" she said, excitedly. "I'll share mine with you."

"Thank you, and I'll share mine with you."

I couldn't take my eyes off the two of them as they interacted for the first time. They seemed so in sync with each other. My eyes watered and I sniffed.

Kane swiveled his head toward me and mouthed, *Are you okay?*

I nodded. "You two are just so beautiful to watch." It took four years, but I finally had my family.

He put his arm around me, tugging me close, and kissed me. Ava giggled. "We're finally a family," he said.

"I was just thinking the same thing."

A car pulled up marked with the FBI logo on the side. A stab of fear went through me.

* * *

Kane

Agent Latasha Watson parked her car and got out. "I didn't do it," I said as she approached.

She smiled and waved at Ava, who had waved at her. "I know. I'm not here for you, but it involves you. Sort of."

"Uh-oh," Jordy said.

"I'm glad I caught you. I wanted to thank you."

"For what? I should be thanking you every day for the rest of my life."

"Ryan passed on the name you gave him to me when he wasn't having any luck."

"And you found something?"

"Yeah, Rodney Javernick doesn't exist," Latasha said.

"Um…" I pursed my lips. Opened my mouth to ask what she was talking about and closed it. *Huh?*

"Rodney Javernick is the alias of someone well-known for his hacking skills. The kind of skills the FBI would be interested in. But no one knew who he really was, or how to find him. The alias is actually the stolen identity of someone who died five years ago. Since Javernick was supposedly a missing person, I checked with the DMV to get his picture and discovered something interesting."

"But I met his dad, Ray Javernick," I said.

She shook her head. "Ray Brock is the trucker you met."

"Sonofab—" Oops, I needed to remember I had an example to set for Ava.

"Anyway, junior's in prison for cybercrimes. And guess what his name is? Then guess his alias."

"Rodney Javernick is—was—my cellmate, Trent Brock. Or Monster, as he's affectionately called." I chuckled.

"Bingo. I interviewed him regarding what happened with Larson, and I noticed he looked familiar. It was the eyes that did it for me. So, I asked him right there if he was Javernick."

"Shit—shoot. I assume Ray knew about the cybercrimes."

"Yep.

"Which is why he was convinced someone had killed him. But he just got caught phishing."

"You guessed it. He had a little cybercrime ring going and got caught. But I can't tell you why he wouldn't tell his father, unless they were estranged."

I remembered something. "I saw his fake ID. The picture looked a lot like me."

"Yeah, he gained about a hundred pounds since the photo was taken. Weight can really alter a person's looks."

She had a point.

"You know, you could have told me or Ryan this over the phone. Why come here?"

"I'm here to offer Brock a job consulting for the FBI. I finally got clearance."

I started laughing. Two favors down: Brock was going to work for the FBI, and Ray had the answer to the mystery of his son's disappearance. But I had an idea in mind for how to repay the last person, Chet the barman, for his kindness. His son wasn't going to like it but fuck him.

Latasha said goodbye and walked into the prison.

Hearing the story about Brock was a surprise. Clearly, Ray Brock had lied about how close he was with his son. Did they even drive a truck together? I thought not.

"What a weird coincidence," Jordy said.

"Yeah, it is." I chuckled. "And I have a feeling I'll be seeing Brock again."

"That wouldn't surprise me for some reason. Did you notice what I'm wearing?"

"Yeah, too many clothes."

Her cheeks flushed. "Not that. You can take them off later, though." She held up her hand, showing me the engagement ring she wore.

"Does this mean you still want to marry me?"

"More than ever."

"In that case…" I set Ava on her feet and got down on one knee. She stayed glued to my side, which made my heart even warmer than it already was. My heart thumped a million miles an hour. Even though I had asked Jordana to marry me before, this was way more special. It didn't matter that we were outside a federal prison, in a cement parking lot with barbed-wire fencing and armed tower guards as a backdrop. We were getting the second chance I never thought would come, and our little Ava was here as a witness. I looked up at Jordy and took her hand. "Jordana Lynn Brooklyn, will you marry me?"

"Yes!"

I surged to my full height, bent her over, and kissed her. The kind of kiss that left us both breathless and wishing we were somewhere private.

There was clapping behind us. The guards who had seen me through the gates were up against it. A few yelled out, "Congratulations," and one shouted, "Get it, Adler!"

I laughed.

Jordy blushed.

And Ava giggled.

After some more "Congrats," we waved and headed for her car.

"You know," I said, "I've been giving a lot of thought to the idea of continuing to tutor inmates for the GED. If they will allow me, I'd like to do that on a volunteer basis, part-time."

"I like that. What are you going to do with the other part of your time?"

"Besides spending time with you and Ava…skydiving instructor."

"Uh, you're kidding, right? You've never even jumped out of an airplane before."

I smiled. "About that…"

ABOUT THE AUTHOR

A.J. Norris writes action-packed, character driven stories. She likes her paranormal and romantic suspense dark and delicious with a touch of humor. Her favorite kind of protagonists are strong heroines who often become their own hero.

A.J. lives in Michigan with her supportive family and two adorable Yorkie mixes.

www.ajnorrisauthor.com